"I s ... to remai ...

"Of ... y, breath ... 's figure ... anyway? Nothing. Merely his outline. So why did she feel as if someone had hit her in the stomach with a brick?

Jeffrey brought the bedding items back to the bed and spread them out, tossing the pillows to Alessandra to arrange down the middle of the bed. She lay back, burrowing under the covers, only her dark-haired head with the little nightcap tied under her chin showing.

"I should have thought to wonder why the servants did not leave the warming pans for the sheets. I cannot imagine why they did not."

"I can. Your father's order, no doubt," Jeffrey grumbled.

Alessandra found herself wondering how many couples had spent a wedding night on this very mattress, and how many of them had shared the spot in the middle, leaving this troublesome dip that she found herself sliding toward.

She tried to find a position that allowed her to hold on to the side of the mattress. "Good night," she said quietly once she thought she had achieved her goal.

"Good *morning*," he said with emphasis.

A June Bride

Teresa DesJardien

ZEBRA BOOKS
KENSINGTON PUBLISHING CORP.

ZEBRA BOOKS

are published by

Kensington Publishing Corp.
475 Park Avenue South
New York, NY 10016

Copyright © 1991 by Teresa DesJardien

First printing: July, 1991

Printed in the United States of America

Chapter 1

Alessandra left the house with Miss Parker in tow, but Miss Parker was long gone by the time the trouble began. Alessandra had not intended to lose her chaperone, but then neither had she intended to wander from her group of acquaintances, only to find herself quite alone on a back path.

It was an extraordinarily fine June day, the kind of day that one often dreamed about but seldom saw in the heart of London so early in the summer. The breeze was clement, the sunshine dazzling, and birdsong filled the air. The park's flowers had opened their buds to the wonder of the day, not unlike the admiring faces of their human visitors, and so it could be completely blamed on the refinement of the day itself that Alessandra's chaperone had failed to notice that they had become separated.

For herself, Alessandra was not unduly upset. She knew that she had only to circulate any number of times before she would find Miss Parker happily engaged over some petal or leaf with her pocket-sized magnifying glass in hand. She only hoped that Miss Parker had not managed to be diverted behind a hedge, for Alessandra was petite of stature, with never a hope of seeing over high shrubberies. This troublesome thought having occurred to her, and after only a moment's hesitation to see that she was indeed quite alone on this lesser-traveled path, she decided to climb somewhat inelegantly atop the nearby retaining wall, the better to gaze about for the missing Miss Parker.

Such was the lovely nature of this fine June morning that even Lord Jeffrey Huntingsley, eldest son of the earl of Chenmarth, who now carried his father's lesser title of Viscount Huntingsley, happened also to be strolling in the park. It was not in the common way of things to see this gentleman walking the park, or indeed for him to be seen about London much at all. He had been sent a summons from his father, and though they were somewhat estranged, it was not in Jeffrey's character to blatantly ignore a request for his presence. The ostensible reason for the summons was that he was to demonstrate his skill at managing the unwieldy combination of both estate books and how those said-same books might be viewed by town barristers. It was not much of an excuse to be summoned forth from the relative pleasures of the country, but Lord Chenmarth was given to odd fits and starts of parental behavior, exercised in any number of curious ways for quite some years now. This being the case, plus the fact that nearly every living creature beyond the livestock had removed themselves from the delights of Kent, Jeffrey allowed himself to be persuaded to come to town.

He was probably the only participant in the day's leisure who was less than satisfied with the beautiful day.

Oh, it was grand to feel the sun on one's face, and the air was that rare and perfect temperature that simply demands a saunter about in it, and he was young, and plump of pocket. He had no real worries, and actually after a fashion anticipated the challenge of demonstrating his knowledge to the barristers long in his family's employ, but yet . . . there was something . . . oh, *melancholy* about the very picture of perfection that surrounded him. Jeffrey Huntingsley never cared much for art that showed divinely gorgeous people sitting about in exquisitely perfect dress and pose. Instead he favored portraits of real faces, with lines in their skin, and one or two hairs out of place, and *real* expressions on their faces, not those high and lofty expressions some artists portrayed so well.

Yet even as he thought idly about these things, his hands casually in his pockets as he wandered absently along, he laughed a little to himself. Surely the vague and unnamed feelings of discontent he knew so often lately had nothing to do with the fineness of the day, and he was a sad and sorry fellow for looking for imperfection whilst he stood amongst Eden. He chided himself silently for a moment, turning down a side path, not even taking note that he had chosen a path that was sure to be less traveled, and therefore conducive to yet another bout of cheerless introspection.

At first he thought he had come into a part of the grounds that hosted a statue, but a second quick glance proved that not only was the statue graced with a pale pink gown and dark, rich hair, but it was also capable of motion. His sudden appearance had obviously startled her, for she visibly jumped. He had only a moment more to realize that this was someone he ought to recognize and whose name he ought to know, when she lost her obvious battle to maintain her balance and fell toward him, one arm windmilling furiously as the other stretched out to break her fall.

She fell heavily onto his chest, knocking him back several paces, her one arm smacking him in the ear painfully. Together they did a strange little waltz, until, after a few very long moments, he managed to get a leg behind himself to thrust in the opposite direction, halting their course abruptly.

There was a very audible rip, which they both responded to by pushing off one another to glance down at their own assorted bits of clothing. There was a price to be paid for the yet again sudden movement, for their horrified glances revealed that his booted foot was clearly standing on the hem of her silken dress, and a second ripping sound pointed out that it was the bodice of her gown that was ultimately suffering the damage. It gaped open by more than a few inches, her corset clearly revealed. She gave a curious sound that was a cross between a squeal and a moan, and breaking from the frozen stance of horror she had obtained, suddenly moved to cover the rend with her arms.

Bright blue eyes flew to his. Alessandra saw before her a tall and handsome gentleman, with eyes that were the most lovely dark brown, and which she suddenly knew would appear almost black in the proper lighting. Another flash crossed her mind, and she recognized the hair, too, that color that is referred to as "sandy," and which had often caused the fellow's parents to quibble back and forth as to whether it was truly blond or brunette. He had grown to full maturity since last they had met—oh, ages ago!—and his height struck her now as being rather remarkable, and the width of his shoulders had surely never been so broad before, but yet she knew him after just a moment's wild stare at his straight nose and not-too-full mouth. "Jeffrey?" she whispered in mortified recognition.

"Alessandra?" he queried, not quite sure for a moment if it was her, or her older sister, the Hamilton girls being so alike. He knew only that he and she were somehow related, perhaps as third cousins or some such. No, this must be the younger one, Alessandra. When was the last time they had met? It must be three years ago. But how she had grown!—in great good looks, if not in height. Her face was dominated by the sparkling blue eyes, surrounded as they were by luxurious dark, long lashes. Her hair had not lightened, had in fact darkened into a rich, full chestnut brown. The small, pert nose he recalled, and the bow mouth still had its dimple when she smiled, and he found himself thinking that here at— what? eighteen years of age or so?—she was every bit as charming as she had shown promise of becoming when she was a child. He found himself wondering how he had ever managed to overlook her at the last family gathering, though he had to concede that the ensuing three years had undoubtedly made a lot of difference. He would have been twenty then, and she fifteen. Now she was nothing less than striking, a fact which, strangely, he found himself thinking was due as much to the lively sparks in those eyes as to the gift of beauty itself.

"Get off my dress!" she wailed when he only stood and stared at her.

Belatedly he moved his foot, and she at once attempted to gather the slippery fabric together over her exposed underthings. Feeling at least partially responsible for the

9

tear to her gown, his hands came up automatically, attempting fruitlessly to make right what had gone wrong. When the edges slipped from under her fingers, his own hands sought to gather up the fabric, a muddled and not-quite-formed thought in his mind being that surely between the both of them they could contrive to arrange the material over the gaping hole well enough to make a hasty escape from the park.

The scuffle of a boot and the swish of a skirt came to them, and both Alessandra and Jeffrey half-turned to see Lord and Lady Graham staring at them. Lady Graham's mouth dropped open, even as her eyes started to roll back in her head, while Lord Graham cleared his throat noisily, his eyes bulging slightly.

"I say—!" Jeffrey cried, as it seemed that Lord Graham had no idea that his wife was about to collapse in a faint. Jeffrey began to step forward in an effort to catch the woman, but as he did so, letting go of Alessandra's gown, the hole gaped open anew. His cousin moaned again, and crossed her arms over her exposed bosom once more. Lord Graham became suddenly aware of his wife's condition when that lady slumped against him heavily.

"What manner of outrage is *this* in a public park?" Lord Graham demanded as the weight of his wife nearly sent him down in a sprawl. "I know you, young lady!" he added, staring accusingly over his prostrate wife's head.

"Oh, Lord Graham! I tore my gown—"

"Tore it! I saw the ruffian there do it. Don't try to tell me otherwise, you little tart!"

"Sir, I respectfully demand that you recall those words," Jeffrey stepped forward threateningly, his eyes open wide with a combination of dismay and ire.

"He is my cousin!"

"I don't care if he's your husband! This kind of behavior does not belong in the King's parks, I tell you. I ought to call the guard!"

"Sir, this is all a simple mistake. . . ." Jéffrey started to explain, but Lord Graham had finally turned his attention to his wife. "Margaret! Margaret? My dear, are you all right?"

Their voices had carried, and other couples began to gather on the off-the-pace walkway. Jeffrey swore under his breath, and removed his coat. He placed it around Alessandra's shoulder, backwards, to cover her ripped gown. *So much for a quiet escape*, he thought.

Someone called for a litter; someone else called for hartshorn to revive the prone Lady Graham. Questions and calls of "what happened here?" flew back and forth, and Jeffrey gritted his teeth against the ludicrous answers that resulted. The whole mad scene was not helped by Lord Graham's strident demands for "decency in the parks," and his claims that he was coming to see Alessandra's father as soon as he could get his wife safely to home and a doctor's care.

Jeffrey put his arm around Alessandra, the better to hold his coat over her, and escorted her past a gauntlet of ogling faces. "Which is your carriage?" he ground out as they came near to the exit from the park.

"The farthest one, there." She indicated the direction with a nod of her head.

"Of course it is," he said from between gritted teeth, and hurried her forward past another sea of gawking observers.

"To the Hall, if you please!" Jeffrey called to the driver curtly as they approached the vehicle.

"'Ere now, 'oo are you? What's wif Miss Alessandra?"

11

the driver demanded in return with a dark scowl.

"Tim, it's all right, he's my cousin. Jeffrey Huntingsley. Surely you know him; Lady Chenmarth's son," she called from her seat to the driver, whom had been in the Hamilton employ for years. "It's all right. Do as he says," she soothed, easing the disapproving frown from his brow.

The driver grunted then, and asked of Jeffrey, "Which 'all then? Yours, or 'ers?" It was not uncommon for Alessandra's family to visit Aunt Jane at Huntingsley Hall.

"New Garden Hall, and hurry if you care for an extra quid!" Jeffrey snapped, climbing in beside Alessandra. As he settled them both on the squabs, he growled, "At least this vehicle's top is up!"

"Oh, Jeffrey, however did that hideous scene ever happen?" she cried, her blue eyes wide with distress.

He gazed at her in return, seeking to control his own upset. A moment more of regarding her and it was clear she was not going to cry, a fact which pleased him, however grimly.

"I'm afraid," he said in a voice that he forced into tones more calm than he felt, "that scene was as nothing compared with what is going to happen when Lord Graham comes to speak with your father."

Alessandra looked at him somewhat blankly as she let his words sink in, but after a moment he saw her eyes grow very wide indeed.

Chapter 2

"I don't care *how* it happened!" Malcolm Hamilton shouted.

Alessandra shivered in the face of her father's rage, Jeffrey's lips thinned even further in vexation, and Alessandra's mother sat very still, her face pale. Miss Parker covered her mouth with her hand and fled the room from her position near the door, obviously thinking to excuse herself from a volatile family matter.

Alessandra watched her chaperone's hasty retreat and wished she could do the same. While she had changed her gown she had only had a few minutes' respite from what she knew could only be her father's upset before Lord Graham had arrived on their doorstep. That interview had been held behind ominously silent doors, and far too quickly ended to promise any forbearance on her father's part. She was developing a powerful headache. She had hoped that once Miss Parker had been retrieved from the park, that lady might shed some helpful light on the subject that was so infuriating Lord Malcolm. Unfortunately Miss Parker's blithesome unawareness of the day's happenings, and the subsequent jumbled versions told thereof to her by several persons with overriding opinions, had only served to further aggravate him.

"Papa, please try to understand—"

"I understand perfectly!" he thundered, the ends of his graying hair trembling with outrage. "I understand that Lord Graham came to my home to inform me that my daughter was seen, unescorted by her chaperone, being disrobed in a secluded walkway in a public park! I understand that Jeffrey was the man doing it! I understand—"

"I was not disrobing your daughter, sir."

"Did you, or did you not, rip her dress?"

"Malcolm, please, don't shout so," Alessandra's mother, Lady Amelia, cried with an eye toward the closed doors where servants' ears probably resided.

"I did, but it didn't happen the way it sounds—"

"I don't care *how* it happened. I *do* care that it *did* happen!" Lord Malcolm made what was only a futile effort to lower his voice, for as he continued it grew in volume again. "What about my daughter, sirrah? What about her? She's ruined, that's what! You know what a nine-day wonder the tattlemongers will make of this!" Lord Malcolm strode back and forth across the carpet, his vivid blue eyes crackling fire, one vengeful hand raised as though he were prepared to smite Old Hickory himself.

"Exactly the point I was trying to make, my lord. It will only be a nine-day's wonder, and then everything will go back to as it was," Jeffrey said calmly, crossing his arms and leaning back against the mantelpiece in a nonchalant attitude that was belied by the tightness of his jaw. He was trying his best to keep his own temper even if Lord Hamilton could not.

14

"It will *not* 'go back as it was'! Lessie there will still be ruined forever. And what are you going to do about that, hmm? Well, I'll tell you what you are going to do! You are going to marry my daughter before these nine days of wonder are over, do you hear me?"

The room fell silent, and they all looked at one another with stricken or shocked faces. Jeffrey stood upright, his arms falling to his sides in astonishment.

"Oh, Papa, no," Alessandra protested weakly.

"You be silent. You've no say in the matter. If you'd wanted say, you should have thought of that before you allowed all this to happen," her father snapped at her.

"I just ripped my dress!"

"Then why did he have his hands all over you? Why were the two of you alone? No, don't say another word! You'll only make matters worse. Amelia, take your daughter up to her room and put her to bed. She's going to be busy tomorrow," he said with ominous promise in his voice. He turned back to Jeffrey, who exchanged glare for equal glare.

Amelia arose and led a protesting Alessandra from the room. She only had time to throw Jeffrey one beseeching look before her mother firmly closed the door between them.

"Come along, Alessandra. I suspect your father is quite right; we should put you to bed," Lady Amelia said, avoiding her daughter's eye and clucking her tongue.

"Mama, you have to persuade Papa that marriage is out of the question. It's ridiculous. I haven't even had my first season yet. I was so looking forward to all the balls and assemblies. I just tore my dress. Yes, I know there was a scene, but I'm sure—"

"Your father will know what is best for you," Amelia said. She had the glint in her eye, the one that said "Father has spoken the eleventh commandment."

When puddles of tears formed anew in Alessandra's eyes, her mother softened just a little, and she put her arm around her daughter's shoulders. "Tut-tut," she soothed. "Really, you must trust your father and me in such a matter. Everything will be made right. Hush now, darling. Come on then, that's a good girl. I'll ring for Patty, and she'll have you tucked in right and tight in two shakes of a lamb's tail. Oh, my darling girl, don't cry. We'll make it all better, you'll see."

And so Alessandra allowed herself to be soothed into bed and into slumber, never dreaming that downstairs the very thing she didn't want to happen had just been arranged.

Alessandra was more or less shoved into the room, the door pulled shut soundly behind her.

"Jeffrey," she greeted her cousin, wincing internally at the stiffness she heard in her own voice.

"Alessandra."

She wondered briefly if she looked as haggard as he did this morning, though she had to concede she had slept well enough last night. It was only her father's firm announcement this morning that she was to consider herself betrothed that had caused the color to fade from her cheeks.

Jeffrey looked as though he had not slept a wink all night. His cravat was simply tied, his eyes were red-rimmed, and his boots reflected the possibility that they had not seen a proper polishing since his walk in the park yesterday.

"You wanted to see me?" she asked, unable to keep the hard-edged tone of trepidation from creeping into her voice, for she knew why he was there and what he was going to say.

"As you probably know, I've come to ask you to be my wife. Will you do me the honor?" he said baldly. He stood with his back to the fireplace, his arms crossed as he gripped each of his elbows. Alessandra fleetingly thought to herself that this was the very look of a belligerent schoolboy made to recite before the class.

She glided across the room, coming to stop in front of him. When she spoke her tone was no longer contentious, softening into something more like anguish. "I . . . I don't know what to say. I mean, I do, for Papa has ordered me to accept. In fact, he says that your asking me is just a formality, and as I am under the age of my majority, I will have to do as he says in any event. But, what I mean is . . . I will find a way to defy him if it will make you miserably unhappy that we wed."

He lowered his eyes for a moment, and she felt a strange little lump begin to form in her stomach. Not that she had expected him to be overjoyed that Papa would settle for nothing less than leg-shackling him to her, but still it hurt to guess she was so repugnant to him as all that.

"It's not a simple matter, Alessandra," he said at length, finally raising his eyes to meet hers.

"Why not? We could just say we won't do it. I'll probably be locked in my room until Papa can whisk me away to rusticate—" she hesitated and chose not to say *forever*"—in the country, but I would truly much prefer that occurrence over causing us both to form a distressing union."

He smiled faintly at her words, thinking that only a girl fresh from the schoolroom could phrase things quite so dramatically, but aloud he said, "In the first place, I am afraid your father may be correct in thinking that this little episode has put you quite beyond the pale. Perhaps if you had already been presented, so that people knew you and your sensibilities a little, then perhaps they could be a trifle forgiving of a little peccadillo—if it could be properly explained.

"In the second place, Lord Graham has been having a marvelously wondrous time dining out about town on the tale. I know this, because I thought for a moment that I was to be refused entrance at my club last night. So you see, it is not only your reputation which suffers, but my own as well."

Alessandra sank down into a chair, her legs suddenly unable to hold her properly. "Oh," she said quietly.

He began to pace the length of the room, his arms akimbo as he spoke.

"However, if we were *not* to marry, you would, as you have mentioned, be sent off to the country. We can only wonder if the locals would querry the fact that the beautiful, dowered girl from a wealthy family is not sent to London to make a debut. It is possible that this would not become an issue, and it is possible that it would not come to the attention of fortune seekers and cits, but I must tell you that your father believes both cases to be highly likely to occur."

She heard what he said, including the fact that he had

called her beautiful. Even in the midst of disaster, she was female enough to enjoy a moment's pleasure at the compliment.

"As for myself, I should be quite surprised to find I was accepted into the home of any mama in London, with the same possible exception of cits and fortune seekers. Since I was not particularly in mind to find a wife just now, this would not unduly upset me, except that I cannot care to inflict the same banishment upon my parents and my brother, Elias."

He stopped and turned to face her, a slight frown settling on his brow. "On the other hand, if we agree to marry, then we each have someone whom we know is not after our funds, titles, or possessions. We know each other, and I am bold enough to suggest we could even like each other a little. We would be accepted into society once again under the blessings of marital propriety."

He looked at her, hard, and then said simply, "So." It was a sort of question, and he waited for her response.

She lifted her hands in a little gesture of resignation, but her words belied the gesture of surrender. "I have one—no, two problems with this 'solution' of Papa's."

"They are . . . ?" he urged her to go on.

"The first is rather silly, I suppose, but it bothers me a great deal." She could not meet his eye, for this was the oddest conversation she had ever had in her eighteen years of life.

"Tell me what it is."

"Well," she started, then had to stop, only to start again. "Well, if we exchange marriage vows," she had to stop again, aware of the flaming red in her cheeks. It seemed such a private thought, and she had never shared a private thought with a man before. She hurried ahead, "It is simply that I should not be comfortable standing before God and swearing that I will 'love, honor, and obey you' if such is not true."

He gazed down at her with his rich, dark eyes, and slowly a kind smile formed across his lips. "You are a very nice girl," he said, startling her with the observation.

He moved to sit next to her. She made room for him, more than was necessary so that even the skirts of her powder blue gown did not touch him, but he moved closer and gathered up one of her hands in his own.

"I think that we can agree if we marry that those words must have a particular, special meaning for us, a cousinly contract, I suppose, as we would agree upon here and now."

He paused to think for a moment, then said, "For us they would mean that we should *love* as best we may, even if it is in only a familial way. And we should *honor* the marriage vows—sickness and health, and all that—and *obey* would mean when and where it applies to the household or the marriage as a union."

"Are you saying . . . that we should live separate lives such as your mother and father do?"

His eyebrows shot up, but his thoughtful smile did not waver. It was certainly no family secret that his mother and father had lived in completely separate households for years now. The entire extended family had felt the social sting that had accompanied the messy separation, and it had certainly served to make family reunions extremely awkward and increasingly infrequent as time marched on. However, the ugliness of the whole affair

20

was in Jeffrey's mind completely dwarfed by the fact that it had been much more unpleasant living in a house where both his antagonistic parents had resided, and he could only think they had been very wise to go their own ways.

"After a fashion, yes. I don't think it would be fair to ask you to . . . to have no lovers, but I would ask that under the 'obey' part of the ceremony, you would be most discreet in any such matter."

She stared at him, unable to hide some of the repugnance she felt at such an offer of husbandly "understanding." She looked away for a moment, and found herself thinking, to her own great astonishment, that it was, in its way, a magnanimous offer, for without such an understanding between them, she would be forced to live a severely sterile life.

She looked back at him sharply the moment she realized the agreement must, of needs, extend to him as well. The very calmness of his expression told her that this was so.

"And what is your second worry?" he asked.

By saying nothing in complaint now, she knew she was tacitly agreeing to his terms, if they were to marry. She was not sure why it bothered her just the faintest measure to think of someone whom she would call "husband" taking lovers for himself, but she comforted herself with the thought that he was promising to be discreet as well. She found herself hoping they had a mutual understanding of the word *discreet*.

"Your second worry?" he urged her again, recalling her from her outlandish thoughts.

"You should be able to guess that!" she more or less

snapped at him, for she had no ability to say what was in her mind, unless he counted her deep blush as words enough.

"Ah!" he said, and his expression grew even more cool. "The conjugal rights, I presume?"

She nodded her head mutely, amazing herself by her own ability to hold up her head and return his gaze.

"I presume you do not care to share them?"

She leaped to her feet, swaying just a little as the blood in her face tried to race to her feet.

He leaped to his feet as well and grabbed her by the forearms to steady her, and his smile had grown bantering. "No, no, I'm only teasing! Forgive me. I have often been accused of introducing humor into conversations where others believe it does not belong."

"I should say so!" she managed to gasp.

"Well, I thought it was obvious, you see. Since we agreed to allow each other to go our own ways, I assumed we were not to practice those familial duties of which we so delicately speak."

She resented the laughter in his tone and in his eyes, and said severely, "*Some* of us speak delicately."

"And some of us know whereof we speak, I believe."

To her horror, his steady look accused her of knowing more of the facts of life than a well-brought-up maiden ought to know, and she knew, miserably, that he could confirm the truth of this by her own telltale blushes.

She sputtered for a moment, wanting to explain that sisters and schoolgirls spoke of these things because they were perceived to be important, and because they were subjects so carefully avoided by their parents, all the while knowing she would look even more hoydenish if she tried to explain.

"It is as well, my dear," he soothed, laughter in his voice yet again. "I should not care for making a bargain where you did not know what you were giving up."

She gasped anew, and stared at him quite frankly. Did he think he was such a wondrous bargain? Why was he teasing her so ruthlessly? If they married, would they go on in this . . . this teasing, *hateful* manner?

These thoughts passed through her mind in a twinkling, followed at once by the echo of him saying he often used humor at odd moments where it might be said it did not belong. Meeting his gaze squarely, she could see that he was teasing himself as much as her.

To her surprise, she found her anger sliding away and she was laughing, and then he was laughing with her.

"Well," he said, shaking his head without losing his grin, "I think we must have struck an accord."

She shook her head as well, still smiling a little, though her voice became meditative as she said, "I believe we have."

"There is nothing left for it then, but to shake on it."

He extended his hand, and she offered her own. His grip was firm, her hand small against his, and with a sigh of mingled amusement and uncertainty she knew her future had been decided.

She watched as he moved her hand from where he clasped it, turning the back of it up, and raised it to his lips. He gave the gallant's kiss, his lips not even really touching her skin. He did not release her hand as he straightened, and his eyes were once again sober as he looked down at her.

"I would clarify one thing."

"Yes?" she said somewhat unsteadily, for courtly gestures, until this moment, were only things that her mother had tried to teach her about. She had found out quite suddenly that they were ever so much more gratifying in reality than they were in practice.

"I would that we will treat each other with respect. Oh, I'm not just speaking of taking lovers, but in all matters. You must know, I was raised in a home where there was constant bickering, and constant pettiness. My parents did their best to misunderstand one another in a hundred spiteful little ways, and often too publicly. It was really for the best when they chose separate homes, as then at last my father had a little heart and energy to bestow upon my brother and myself. And we could visit mother in a home that had some semblance of peace to it.

"So, although as newlyweds we must make the effort to reside together at first, I do not care to live in such a strife-filled home. If we find we cannot live together peacefully, I would ask that we do as my parents have done."

He still held her hand, perhaps a little too hard, so that she had the distinct impression that this was very important to him. Her young, sweet heart felt for his suffering in years past, and she answered readily, "Of course. I, too, could not care to live where there is no harmony."

"Thank you," he said quietly, raising her hand once more for the gallant's kiss.

The double doors of the front parlor swung open wide, and in marched a pretty lady still clad in her traveling clothes, her features suspiciously like Alessandra's. "Well?" she demanded, her hands on her hips, her pelisse winding around her skirts in a swirl of activity

24

that indicated she had wasted no time entering the room.

Jeffrey looked at the woman, at Alessandra's delight-edly welcoming face, and then back at the other woman, whom he finally recognized. "Cousin Emmeline!"

She ignored him and marched up to her little sister, her expression demanding an immediate answer.

"Emmeline, you know Jeffrey . . ." Alessandra said, her voice a mixture of shyness and a funny kind of pride as she added, "My betrothed."

"Well done!" Emmeline cried in her resonant fashion as she broke into smiles, and proceeded to hug them both at once.

Chapter 3

"Father. Elias," Jeffrey said over the dinner table. Their plates were satisfactorily empty, but Jeffrey's plate was still full, however pushed about the food had been. They looked at him as he spoke, their mutually steely gray eyes (so appropriate in his sober father and so unsuitable for lighthearted Elias) now somnolent over the pleasant repast they had just enjoyed.

Jeffrey cleared his throat, and seeing he had even managed to attract the butler's attention, he waved the fellow out. When the servant was gone, he went on, "I have something I must tell you. I do hope you will not be unduly upset, and that you will be aware that the situation was not precisely of my making."

Elias set down his wine glass and regarded his older brother with a renewed measure of interest. It was so rare to see Jeffrey discomfited. His older brother usually had an irrepressible wit, perhaps less nonchalant than Elias's own, yet consistently at the ready. Whatever his big brother was about to say, it could only be monumental in its import, to judge from the lack of lightness in his tone.

"I became betrothed today," Jeffrey said, his chin buried into his cravat. Without looking up, he hastily added, "but not to Jacqueline Bremcott."

His father, Richard Huntingsley, the recently named earl of Chenmarth, choked on his wine and coughed for a full minute before he recovered himself.

Elias looked to his brother, his father's slightly purple face, then to Jeffrey again, his eyes wide and filled with animation. "I say, good show!" he called out, for it had never been any secret that Elias had not cared overmuch for the thought of Jacqueline Bremcott becoming his sister-in-law.

"Who? Who is the girl?" his father demanded sharply as soon as he could speak.

"She is . . ." Jeffrey found himself floundering for a moment, but her name came to him after only a moment, ". . . Alessandra Hamilton."

"Malcolm's youngest girl?" his father asked, sitting back with a furrowed brow, a finger coming up to rub along the side of his nose. It was immediately evident he was shocked but not dismayed, as he had been prepared to be.

"Little Lessie Hamilton?" Elias hooted, slapping the table delightedly with one hand.

"She is not so little now. Eighteen . . . or so I would have to venture a guess," Jeffrey grumbled, still not wanting to meet their eyes, least of all his carefree, careless brother's.

The room fell silent, and Jeffrey was just on the verge of rising from his chair to make an escape, when his father leaned forward on his elbows, his chin coming to rest on his intertwined fingers. He said in his sternest paternal voice, "All right then, Master Jeffrey. We all, including *you* I believe I may say, thought to see you one day offer for Jacqueline. This sudden engagement to Alessandra is too unexpected to not have a tale behind it. We'll have the whole of that tale out of you, if you please."

Without the constant interruptions and heightened dramatics that had occurred at Alessandra's home, his story was soon clearly retold. He could tell by their expressions that Elias was pleased and vastly amused, but a glance at his father showed him that Lord Richard was less in charity over the matter.

"Well! I can only imagine what Letitia Bremcott will have to say to this!" Lord Richard said with an anticipatory shudder of having to meet up with the lady. "After all, there has been an understanding for these ages past."

"That is not precisely true, Father. You and Lord Bremcott had an understanding, and he passed away years ago. And, I might add, that understanding was made when Jackie and I were only babes. And she and I have never actually spoken toward the matter," Jeffrey denied quickly. At his father's openly skeptical look, he sat up straight in his chair, using his hands for emphasis as he went on, "Yes, it was assumed we would eventually make a pact of it one day, but you will recall that Jacqueline made her debut last year. I fully anticipated that she would bring some other, er, lucky fellow up to scratch . . . and since that was not the case, it has furthermore become clear to me that she intended another season and another try."

"Jeffrey! I'll have you know that Jacqueline Bremcott discouraged a viscount, waiting for your offer. And it wasn't just a courtesy title like yours neither. Her mother told me so herself!"

"Jeffrey will be an earl one day. Jacqueline knew what she was doing," Elias put in.

He was soundly rapped on the knuckles by his father's soup spoon for his efforts. "Ouch!" he cried as he rubbed his offended knuckles, but he continued to smile in a way his parent could only think of as unpleasant.

"Elias!" Lord Richard snapped, "you are excused."

"I'm not a child."

"Then stop acting like one. This is serious, and we'll have none of your flippancy."

"I can't help m'self. Jackie's a nice enough girl, but can you possibly picture her with Jeffrey? They would become the stuffiest couple on Earth."

"I said you were excused," Lord Richard said slowly, fixing not one but two steely eyes on his younger son.

"Oh, very well." Elias stood and made a half-bow to the table at large. As he passed behind his brother's chair, he clapped him quickly on the shoulder, and said in a perfectly audible voice, "In my room. Later."

Jeffrey did not acknowledge the comment.

Lord Richard took a deep breath which he released as a long sigh. His sandy locks were worn a little longer than was the current fashion, his eyes so unlike the doelike dark brown that Jeffrey had inherited from his mother. It was, however, manifestly evident from whom Jeffrey had inherited his height and build, as well as his hair coloring. Lord Richard, at age fifty, was still a decidedly handsome man, giving his son every hope of aging equally as gracefully.

But now his father's fine features looked rather pinched as he sighed and said, "Well, my lad, there's nothing for it, no matter how a man looks at it. Any understandings with the Bremcotts aside, you'll have to marry the Hamilton girl. Can't see any way around it."

"The thing is that I was trying to be honorable. I was trying to assist her. We are cousins, after all. Shouldn't there be some leniency between cousins?" Jeffrey also sighed.

"Not, I am afraid," his father said with the ghost of a smile, "when it involves revealed undergarments in public places."

"You know how that—"

"Oh, don't get in high dudgeon with me! I see the story in its entirety well enough. Still, there's no way to save the girl's name and reputation without continuing to do 'the honorable thing.' She's got money and looks, so really, it should not be such a terrible hardship. Why, both my sisters had arranged marriages, and they turned out right and fine enough. It's the way of the world, you know, and there's a lot to be said for it," he finished his summation with a lifting of his strong chin, so that Jeffrey could see that he was convincing himself as much as his son of the truth whereof he spoke. He did not mention his own arranged marriage, each knowing full well that it had *not* turned out right and fine enough.

"You'll have to tell her," Lord Richard stated.

"Tell who?" Jeffrey asked. "Alessandra? She already—"

"Jackie Bremcott, of course. It would not be kind to let her hear it from the tattlemongers, or to read the banns in the papers."

"There won't be any banns. Not enough time," Jeffrey waved the thought away.

Lord Richard looked shaken for a moment, but then he pushed back his chair and brusquely said, "Quite right. I'm sure Lord Hamilton wants this all wrapped up right

31

and tight as soon as possible. I must go to him now; between us we should contrive to come up with a special license. In three days hence too soon?" he asked, coming to his feet.

"Decidedly," Jeffrey said, paling a little.

"Hmph, my boy! Don't look to me or anyone else to blame for the bed you now find yourself having to lie in, if you'll pardon the pun. 'Twasn't I who went down a side path with an unchaperoned young lady."

"I didn't go down the path *with* her—"

"Tut, no excuses. I'm off to Malcolm Hamilton's now. And don't forget to call on Jacqueline. Without delay!" Lord Malcolm ordered over his shoulder as he went purposefully from the room.

Jeffrey groaned, and leaned his head against the high-backed chair. He closed his eyes, only to snap them open when a hand touched his shoulder.

"Jeffrey! I could not wait upstairs. I eavesdropped and heard it all; no reprieve for the Right Honorable the Viscount Huntingsley, poor sot!" Elias grinned down at him, then moved to take a chair next to his brother's.

"You are incorrigible," Jeffrey frowned at him, but not very severely.

"I can afford to be. Younger son, and all that."

"You'd be the biggest brat alive if you were the eldest son."

"True, true, and so we see how nature balances things for us. Take this engagement to Lessie Hamilton. Now there's a girl with some life in her, perfect for you, not all insipid and proper like Jackie Bremcott."

"I thought you liked Jacqueline."

"I do, at least well enough. She's a fine girl, but there's nothing terribly original about her, is there? She's the kind of girl *I* should marry, to keep me in line, you see. Not that I ever would, mind you. Now you, if you married her, you'd both end up like dried-up old sticks, never a new or interesting thought to be shared between the two of you." He grinned widely at Jeffrey, nodding his head with complete confidence in his own opinion.

"Alessandra is pretty much of the same mold, my dear boy," Jeffrey said languidly to disguise the fact he was faintly intrigued by his brother's observations.

"Oh, she's a proper one, and all that, but she . . . oh, how does one say it? She *sees* things clearly. When she talks, she actually means what comes out of her mouth. She'd never tell you she likes your waistcoat when in truth she thinks it a fright. And she would manage to let you know in the kindest manner possible somehow, nicely, so you'd not feel like you'd made a cake of yourself."

"And how do you know so much of 'Lessie,' as you are wont to call her?" he asked, his voice drawling slightly, whether in amusement or something else, Elias would have liked to know. He eyed his big brother for a minute speculatively, then answered easily, "She's closest of all the cousins to my age. We always romped around together at those family gatherings, while our elder siblings looked down their noses at us. We talked. We played games. I've always found her to be a good gel. I've always liked her."

Jeffrey "hmphed," then sighed and rolled his eyes toward the carved and gilded rococo ceiling over his head as he announced, "I've got to go tell Mother next."

"Horrors!" Elias cried with a mock shudder.

"My sentiments exactly. I cannot care to have a peal rung over my head."

33

Elias, unable to sustain silence or even a shred of respectful sympathy, could not resist torturing his big brother by beginning to hum the "Wedding March."

"Shut your trap," Jeffrey snapped.

"My trap was not open."

"Quit your humming."

"Is it the melody which perturbs you? You'd better get used to it, old boy."

Jeffrey chose to give Elias no further satisfaction on that score. Instead, some of the caution slipped away from his carefully arranged features, and he found himself asking, "Do you find her pretty?"

Elias managed to not grin any more widely, but his voice was smooth as silk when he answered, "A beauty!"

"Yes, she is rather, isn't she?"

They finally allowed themselves to look directly into each other's eyes. Though their dispositions were far from being alike, instead of having been brothers who hated each other all during their youthful years, they had been grand companions. They had shared every kind of adventure, and knew each other well, the friendship they had formed spilling over naturally into adulthood. And now, looking at each other, they could only see in each other's eyes how nearly inconceivable it was that Jeffrey, the responsible elder brother, should find himself in the position of having—however unintentionally—compromised a girl into marriage. The thought flashed between their interlocked eyes, held and twisted between them tautly, until suddenly there was no stopping their instantaneous and mutual shouts of laughter. Elias hooted, unable to do aught but hold his side and shake with laughter, without bothering to wonder if he was offending his big brother, who, it must be said, held on to the edge of the table as he himself giggled helplessly.

The servants were not shocked when, after all these years of similar occasions, a few minutes later they saw the two young masters, aged twenty-three and twenty, running up the stairs. The elder was threatening the younger with imminent and dastardly deaths of all manner and kind, the sum of which were, however, related in the most jovial fashion imaginable.

"But . . . but, Jeffrey!" Jacqueline said, a sob in her throat, tears threatening to spill from her eyes. He gritted his teeth, hoping she would not cry. Alessandra had not cried, not once, to his immense relief. He could be nonchalant as long as a woman did not cry, but when they did he wanted nothing so much as to get up and run in the opposite direction.

"I'm sorry," he said, not exactly sure why he was apologizing, "but it must be this way, you must see that." He had gone through a scene with his mother, Lady Jane Chenmarth, just an hour earlier. She had not appreciated being "one of the last to know." He was not sure he was up to yet another scene now, though there was something to be said for getting all the unpleasantness out of the way in one day. But at least his mother had only scolded him, not resorting to this bothersome business of tears.

"I do. I mean, I understand why Lady Hamilton's father feels the way he does, but . . . oh, Jeffrey!"

Though he had seen it coming, it was to his chagrin that she began to weep.

"Jacqueline, it is not as though this will reflect on you in any way," he said, resisting his natural inclinations by putting a comforting arm around her shoulders and pulling her to a settee.

"But I've told all my friends!"

She realized at once by the stiffness that came into his touch and the way he said "Oh, have you then?" that she had revealed an unflattering and unmaidenly presumption. She quickly amended, "What I mean to say is, I've hinted that I would not have the Viscount Aldegard because my papa wishes that certain estates be joined," she cried into a handkerchief that she pulled unceremoniously from his jacket pocket.

Jeffrey compressed his lips, frowning at his soon-to-be-ruined handkerchief.

He had grown up with the idea that he was to offer for Jacqueline. It had been, in their mutual parents' estimation, a gracious happenstance (that was quite possibly arranged by the Supreme Being) that not only the country but also the town estates shared so conveniently adjoined, albeit accidental, borders. It was evident to all that those estates ought to be engaged in one big happy union.

Although it was equally evident to Jeffrey as well, the traitorous thought had run unbidden any number of times through his head that he did not care one whit whether the properties were joined or not, and he had been putting off that union in all contentment, despite his mother's occasional pointed questions of the last two years. Perhaps this was because it had always seemed so inevitable, but at any rate it piqued him a little to think that this remaining separation of the estates might be Jacqueline's sole objection to his marrying another.

Still, obviously he must not leave her until she had derived some measure of peace of mind, and toward that purpose he spoke. "No banns were posted, no engagement parties thrown. No one will think anything of the fact that I am to marry another. She *is* my cousin, you know, removed a few times. In fact, I'm not quite sure how we're related, but we're not first cousins at any rate. 'Tis not so strange to marry one's cousin. No one will think a thing of it, not in connection with you." His words were abrupt.

Jacqueline, never one to be thought of as slow, heard his tone, and consequently gave another sob, one that allowed her to lean into his chest, the very picture of distressed femininity seeking comfort. She had known him forever, and she knew how and when to retreat to a safe position behind his chivalrous manners. As she had thought it would, his arm came a little more tightly about her shoulders, so that she saw her actions had their desired effect of turning away his anger.

"Jeffrey . . . darling . . ." she said in a low voice, turning her head up so that her face was not far from his. "If this terrible tragedy had not happened, would you have asked me to marry you?"

He stared down into her pixieish face with the wide green eyes, the straight little nose, the sweet kiss of a mouth, all surrounded by a bounty of thick blond hair cut into the latest mode of short riotous curls, and decided it would do no harm to tell her he was more certain of this question than he would have said he was only two minutes earlier had she asked him then. "That was my plan," he said with a less than completely convincing expression, one she apparently failed, or chose not to, observe.

"Oh, darling! You have made me so happy!"

"I—but . . . ! Have you forgotten . . . ?"

"Oh, don't you see? It is so obvious! Of course you must *marry* the girl, but there is nothing in this world that says you must *stay* married to her! The very minute you are married, you must start proceedings to obtain—"

"A *divorce?* Never! Mama would never recover from the shock!" he cried with real feeling.

"An annulment. *Annulment*, silly."

"Well, I . . . I have no idea if that can be done . . . ?"

"Papa says there was a man in his unit who never . . . well, that is to say, he was never a husband to his wife, in the marital way, if you see what I mean," she said quickly, twin spots of color staining her cheeks. "All you have to do is, well, remain chaste, and you may obtain an annulment on those grounds. I daresay the Hamilton girl would be happy enough to arrange it all thusly. You say you do not love her, and neither does she love you, and that both your hands are being forced. So what is to keep you from marrying her to save her name, and then annulling the marriage, so you can be unfettered once again?" She stopped breathlessly, a dazzling smile coming to her well-shaped lips at her own clever foresight.

He continued to stare down at her. For a moment he was tempted to laugh. He would never have guessed there were so many young ladies in London who knew so much of the realities of married life, but then again he had to acknowledge that the pursuit of a husband was paramount in the minds of most whom he had known. Perhaps the topics of bedroom affairs and annulments and nonconsummations had become as *au courant* for young ladies as was the delightfully shocking wetted underthings that drew attention to the forms beneath their gowns.

He tried to bring his thoughts back into order, only to find that his head felt as if it were spinning. Perhaps she was right, perhaps he need not be encumbered for more than a few weeks, or mayhap a couple months at most . . . ? Between the influence of his family and the Hamiltons, and the correct set of conditions such as Jacqueline had suggested, it was surely an obtainable goal. It would neatly solve everything. Hadn't he and Alessandra agreed that theirs was to be a nonphysical alliance? They had said each might have lovers, and had agreed to forego the conjugal rights. The groundwork for nonconsummation was already laid, so why not turn it to the advantage of both? Society's matrons could not disapprove of a dissolution handed down by the Church, and therefore Alessandra would be free to have her first season after all, surely. The same lack of censure would apply to himself and could in no way displease his parents, since it would leave him free to marry another and beget more Chenmarth/Huntingsley heirs. Everyone could walk away with their honor, propriety, and *freedom*, all with only a short period of inconvenience.

"Yes, I see . . ." he murmured, and Jacqueline's smile grew even more bright as she saw acceptance dawn in his eyes.

It was not until he was out on the street, about to take up the reins of his curricle, that it suddenly struck him that he had, more or less, agreed to marry Jacqueline once he was free of Alessandra.

There was a funny feeling in the pit of his stomach, one that he could only assume must be from relief.

Chapter 4

The night before the wedding, Emmeline slipped into her sister's room. "I wanted to talk with you, alone," she said as her younger sister raised an inquiring face to see who had entered without bothering to knock.

"Oh?"

"I see you are putting the final stitches on Mama's gown." They had found some minor repairs needed to be done to the old wedding dress and veil, and Emmeline had clucked a little over the old-fashioned peplum, but in the end all had agreed that, with a few clever stitches, the lovely old lace and satin suited her in both color and styling.

"I want to look well tomorrow. Imagine me, a June bride," Alessandra said, her cheeks pinkening just a little at the renewed thought that tomorrow she was to be married. What an incredible thought! Her marriage had not been even a thought only less than a week ago, and yet tomorrow she must promise to live with a man for the rest of her life.

"You'll be lovely! I daresay it is as well the fabric

41

yellowed a little, for that off-white shade suits you to a tee."

Alessandra ducked her head, not quite willing to show her sister the self-indulgent pleasure she took at this transforming of herself into a bride. She caught a movement in the mirror across from where she sat on the bed, saw her own reflection out of the corner of her eye, saw the long, dark hair, saw what she thought of as the not unpretty face, recognized the glow that she had seen in the faces of other brides. It was very exciting to be the center of attention, very titillating to think of starting on a whole new phase of life. And then she surprised herself when she realized she was trying to guess whether Jeffrey would notice how well she had managed to prepare for their hasty wedding day.

Emmeline stood back, smiling a little as she watched the daydreams dance across her sister's face. Finally, though, her own dreams could not be kept to herself. "I have a little secret," she said in carefully hushed tones, taking advantage of their mother's absence.

Alessandra spun around to face her sister, her hands coming together in a gesture of petition as she cried, "Are you increasing?"

Emmeline could only nod, tears of happiness coming at once to her eyes.

Alessandra threw her arms around her. "Am I the first to know?" she cried. "Of course I am! Mama would be so happy she'd forget all about this wedding!"

"You are the first to know, after James of course," she said, speaking of her husband.

"Oh, I am sure he is delighted!"

"He is!" Emmeline said, beaming brightly. She caught up her little sister's hand, and chided her gently, "But not a word, now, to anyone. I want you to shine all through your wedding day. There's plenty of time for them to spoil me silly after that."

"Oh, Emmy, I am so happy for you!"

"As I am for you. Jeffrey Huntingsley is a very nice man. I know you two will manage to advantage."

Alessandra's smile faded a little as she sat back, a pensive look coming across her features. She half-shrugged and said, "Oh, it's not that way with us, as you know."

Emmeline put her head to one side, a shadow crossing over her features.

"Do you want a girl or a boy?" Alessandra asked abruptly. For reasons she was not quite sure of herself, she felt it was time to change the subject back to her sister, away from this sudden, unplanned wedding.

"Two of each. But one at a time," Emmeline smiled. "In fact, it is on the topic of babies that I am here now."

"Oh?"

"Yes. You see, Mama will feel it is her solemn maternal duty to talk to you tonight, and fill your head with a bunch of fanciful, illogical, scatterwitted comments concerning the way it is between a man and his wife."

"I am not entirely unaware of . . . things."

"'Twas probably I who taught you most of what you already know, but I wanted to be quite sure you understood, because I guarantee that if you do not, then Mama will manage to quite confuse you," Emmeline said, smiling softly to herself to recall some of the misinformation she had had to struggle past.

"Oh, I don't think—" she had meant to say "that it will really be necessary," but Emmeline interrupted.

"It cannot hurt you to listen to me, can it?"

"No, I suppose not," Alessandra said meekly, realizing that she did not really want to explain to her sister that there was not going to be any 'blessed union,' not with Jeffrey, not with her husband. She supposed she should listen, just in case she ever felt she could step aside from her upbringing and actually take a lover, though there was a sour feeling in the pit of her stomach at the very thought of such a thing.

With a feeling rather as though she were eavesdropping, she leaned forward to glean whatever bits of wisdom her sister had to share about the physical union of man and woman.

"Mama will tell you that you should never open your eyes . . ." Emmeline began.

". . . And be sure you never open your eyes. You would not want him to think you have anything of the wanton about you," her mother said, breathing a sigh of relief that she had at last come to the end of her motherly speech.

"Yes, Mama," Alessandra murmured. She raised a hand to her mouth as though to cover a cough, but in truth she was hiding a smile. Emmeline and Mama's accounts had been as far apart in meaning and substance as chickens were from pigs.

She stood, turning her back to her mother, crossing to look out the window of her room that looked down into the kitchen gardens and across the yard that led directly into the stables. It was growing very late, so that moon shadows crisscrossed the neatly arranged rows below. Her smile faded a little, and was replaced by a crease between her delicate dark brows. Surely she and Jeffrey had agreed that he was not to expect these things of her?

It was clear that Mama and Emmeline thought he would, that he had every right to do so, but they did not know about the agreement she and Jeffrey had made.

But, then again, he was marrying her, was he not? Did, then, his discussions of lovers and the special meaning of their vows mean more than she had thought at the time? What did the phrase 'conjugal rights' mean, anyway? What, and how much, had he thought he was giving up? Did he mean he could still expect to produce heirs from their union? No, surely if he had wanted to lie with her for the purpose of progeny, if not that of actual affection, he would have made that a clear part of the bargain . . . wouldn't he have? Yet, without a doubt a wife was for the begetting of the next generation. Affection, desire, passion—those were the things they must take from their lovers. That was surely what he had meant . . . or was it? No, surely he had been clear enough. If he had been concerned about heirs, he would have said something. Though she did not know him well, she had already had enough of his company to feel confident he would have spoken directly to the point.

But if he came to her later, explaining otherwise, could she lie with him? Could she bear it, knowing as she did the hollowness behind it? What was this strange quaking in her limbs; was it fear, was it longing, was it anger?

Her lips drawn grimly tight, she contemplated the two women's separate accountings: Mama had made love-making sound like a duty that resulted in the joy of offspring and family harmony, whereas Emmeline's version had sounded rather a bit like an adventure, an exploration of the heart: yours and his. Emmeline and James had been very evidently in love, as certainly Mama and Papa had been. No, she could not lie with any man, not

45

without love, of that she was sure. Still, it made her feel somehow . . . empty . . . that she was not to know this experience for herself.

"Mama?"

"Yes, my dear?" Her mother crossed to stand behind her, wrapping an arm around her petite daughter's waist over the nightrobe she wore.

She glanced up into her mother's caring face, and away again. "Do arranged marriages really ever work out? Emmeline's was not arranged. Yours was not arranged." She said this almost as an accusation.

"No, not exactly arranged, but our families made a point of throwing us together, so you see we had family blessings from the start. That makes it much easier, all by itself. And you have those very same blessings, Alessandra. But, yes, to answer your question, I've known many an arranged marriage that worked out very nicely." She reached out to gather her daughter's long dark hair in her hands, and began braiding it for the night. "Are you sure you do not care to have your hair cut short?" she asked in that dreamy sort of night voice mothers always use.

"Yes, I am sure. But, Mama, did those people in arranged marriages ever . . . love . . . each other, in time?"

Her mother paused for a moment, then went on braiding. "Well, I suppose, yes, some of them did. And some of them learned to rather like one another, or learned how to go on peacefully. You'll find a way to go on with Jeffrey, my dear, never fear."

So saying, her mother tucked her into bed, kissed her fondly on the forehead and bade her a good night's sleep. "Bright and early tomorrow morning, you'll be a bride!"

she called as she pulled the door shut.

As if she needed reminding, Alessandra thought with a dark scowl.

She thought about her mother's words, her promise that she would find a way to go on with Jeffrey, and she wondered if she would, or if she would end up a part of one of those couples for whom everyone quietly felt sorry. She did not know much, but she did know that she could not be a part of anything like that, not without becoming very hurt, very bitter.

So then, what would be worse? To be left entirely alone with no kind of intimacy at all, or to be only loved in a physical way? Would she and Jeffrey ever find a way to be together? And how much of themselves would they have to give away to achieve a semblance of togetherness?

Chapter 5

"Oh dear, he is wearing gray! Lady Jane distinctly told me Jeffrey was going to wear dark blue."

"Mama," Emmeline chided, rolling her eyes at her little sister as if to say "ignore her!"

Alessandra peeked around the corner of the doors leading from the antechamber into the church, just long enough to try and take a quick peek at her groom. There was a confusion of males near the altar. She saw Mr. Ebey, Jeffrey's best man, whom she had met at the formal betrothal party dinner last night, and whom Jeffrey had introduced as a fellow classmate and good friend from Cambridge. She saw her own little brother, Oliver, so sweet in his finery, though he would not have appreciated being called "sweet" at what he thought of as the advanced age of thirteen. She saw her father, motioning silently and with great exaggeration at someone for some purpose she could not divine, but she could not make out Jeffrey in the moment her head was allowed to show around the door.

"Get back!" Emmeline hissed sternly, pulling her back

by the arm. "No one is supposed to see the bride before the ceremony. *I'll* look."

She did so, and returned to the bride's side to report, "He looks quite dashing. Gray is fine, probably better than dark blue. Blue can be so somber. This is a wedding, after all, Mama."

"But I ordered that dark blue linen be laid for the luncheon!" Lady Amelia almost wailed.

"Perhaps I could change into my blue sarcenet for the luncheon?" Alessandra suggested.

"Why, yes, of course! Although it is not strictly new and it is not *dark* blue, I think if I get out Aunt Agatha's sapphires for you to wear, that would do very nicely. You can save your new rose gown for the going-away trip."

"Going-away trip?" Alessandra echoed faintly. It had not occurred to her that she might be traveling. It had never been mentioned.

Her mother was the picture of guilt. "Well . . . ! I . . . ! Never mind about that now. Oh, there! There is the music. Where is your father?! Oh, goodness gracious me."

That honorable lord came scurrying down the aisle of the church, his gray-streaked hair flying a little in the rush of air he created. He had his son Oliver in hand, and immediately sent that worthy fellow forward with his mother on his arm. He himself had just enough time to catch his breath and to gather up his daughter's hand on his arm before it was their turn to step out into the aisle.

"I was making sure the groom was here. And sober," he whispered in an aside to Alessandra.

"Never say he was drunk!" Alessandra hissed in alarm.

Every head, and there were a surprising many on such

50

short notice, that had not already turned in their direction did so now at the sharp sound.

"No, no, not at all. Just making sure, don't you know. It wouldn't be the first time at a wedding like this."

He felt her little hand relax on his arm, and he whispered one last admonition, "Smile!"

She responded at once, for it was easy to do so. She always smiled like a fool when she was nervous.

Jeffrey looked down the aisle at his approaching bride, for a moment stunned by her transformation. Her lustrous hair had been pulled back and bound in some way, probably into a chignon behind the Juliet cap and veil she wore. Her face, always pretty, was now positively stunning, as her high cheekbones and the ideal angle of her jawline were exposed. Her long dark lashes, framing her glittering blue eyes, were made all the more colorful by the plain ivory hue of the satin gown with its overlay of lace. He saw that her lips were the perfect pink of a rosebud, very flattering to her complexion. He had never really thought about the fact he was at least a head taller than she, but now, in her bridal gown, her diminutive size was brought home to him. He noted, though, that the gown revealed a figure of womanly proportions: breasts that were high and well-rounded, and a diminutive waist that led the eye on to hips of just the right dimensions for balance.

He frowned quickly to himself, chastising himself for making these assessments, and turned his eyes away to stare fixedly toward a stained-glass window on the side wall.

When her father stepped away from her at the altar, she thought for a panicky moment that her legs were going to go out from under her, but then Jeffrey's arm was there, and she clung to him as though he were a life-line.

Together they kneeled before the vicar. She was ashamed to think Jeffrey must be able to feel her trembling, but there was nothing she could do to prevent it. She couldn't even raise her eyes to meet his. What was she doing here? Why was she marrying him? Who was this man, so apparently unruffled, kneeling beside her before God and this entire assembly? Her thoughts chased each other around in her head, until suddenly she realized she was being addressed.

". . . Do you, Alessandra Winifred Hamilton, promise to love, honor, and obey your husband, Jeffrey, until death do you part?" the vicar intoned with his eyes fixed on the Good Book before him. When she did not answer at once, he looked up over the Bible and the pince-nez balanced on his nose, and harumphed discreetly.

In the third row, sitting directly behind Jeffrey's family members, Jacqueline held her breath. The girl, this Alessandra, was hesitating. This girl, so pretty in the lovely lace gown, the cleverly flattering veil, her face charmingly flushed: was she going to call a halt to the proceedings?

Alessandra stared back at the vicar, until finally her eyes, as if of their own volition, raised to meet Jeffrey's. His face was arranged along somber lines, but there was a light of amusement and comprehension in the back of his eyes. His other hand came down on hers where she held his arm and he squeezed gently. It was as if he were saying, "Remember what we agreed: to love, honor, and obey as best we may, respectful of one another." But, too, there was something else . . . no, she had imagined it. He was calm, he was assured; she must emulate him in that.

In fact, he was dashedly handsome. She had always known that her cousin was good-looking, but here, today, in a man's wedding finery, his cravat starched and arranged in clever folds, his rich brown eyes complemented by the gray morning coat and the gray and lilac waistcoat he sported, she saw that he was decidedly attractive.

The vicar cleared his throat again.

Alessandra recalled herself and squeezed lightly on Jeffrey's arm in return. Her voice barely quivering, she answered, "I do."

There were a series of sobs from those who had come to observe the impetuous wedding, and only a few noticed that one of them came from Jacqueline Bremcott.

Alessandra repeated all the phrases every young girl had memorized by heart by the time she was ten: "in sickness and in health"; "for richer, for poorer"; "for better, for worse." Jeffrey was then asked the same questions, and answered each also, "I do."

"You may kiss the bride," the vicar said, beaming down at them as he snapped the Bible closed.

Jeffrey rose to his feet and pulled Alessandra up after him by both hands. He leaned forward and kissed her quickly, his lips striking her on the side of the mouth instead of directly on her lips.

One part of her heard her mother blowing her nose and murmuring, "My baby. My baby,"; another part heard her father telling someone, "All done up then, and didn't cost me a fortune to pop her off, neither!"; and yet another part of her could do nothing but stand there and marvel at the sensation that tingled at the corner of her mouth.

A tug on her arm persuaded her to move, and she came out of her daze to realize that Jeffrey was trying to lead her from the church.

"There's to be a reception," she said to him, and then winced at her own inanity.

"At the house. Yes, I know. Are you all right?" His hand slid under her elbow, the better to steady her.

"Oh, yes, fine." She shook her head, as though to clear it, and managed a smile. "How are we to get there?"

The look he gave her said that she was still saying inane things, but he answered, "The carriage. Your father provided one for us. His party will be brought back with some of the others."

"Oh, the carriage," she said, her smile growing even brighter to cover up the fact that she had almost said, "Alone? Just the two of us?"

He stopped in the antechamber, and she was grateful when she felt the cool stones of a wall pressed against her back: they would help her stay upright.

"Are you going to be all right if I leave you here for a moment? I really should slip a little something to the vicar. I doubt anyone else will recall to do so." He looked at her keenly, but then a flood of well-wishers surrounded them, coming suddenly from the interior church. He seemed to assume that she would be taken care of then, no matter what happened, and so he disappeared back the way they had just come.

"You look so lovely, my dear, truly you do," someone close by said.

By the time Jeffrey returned, ushered through the press by a swell of good wishes, Alessandra had regained her equilibrium. It had helped to have everyone tell her she was beautiful, to fuss over her, and since they all knew exactly why the precipitate wedding had gone forth, tactfully no one asked awkward questions.

"Shall we go?" Jeffrey said, taking her hand and pulling her through the crowd without really waiting for an answer. "Back to New Garden Hall, everyone, for a luncheon and champagne!" he called out, and was promptly cheered by all the men and not some few of the ladies.

After that first paralyzing shock had worn off, Alessandra found herself to be having a wonderful time. She and her groom were toasted and teased, petted and pampered. Her glass was kept filled with champagne, until she finally had to ask that it be taken away altogether else she would become drunk at her own wedding. Her plate was filled and brought to her where she sat at one end of the main dining table. Jeffrey was at the other end, much too far away for conversation, but there were plenty of others to regale her with wild and humorous tales that had her laughing until she begged them to stop. All the young bucks quibbled over who was to stand up with her for the next dance, and they tried to outdo one another in the extravagance of their compliments, for a new bride could be safely flirted with. Her mother's jewels flashed on her throat and in her hair, and a fine gold and diamond wedding band graced her left hand. Her father, during the lull after the first set of dances, guided her about the ballroom, introducing her to his cronies with great aplomb and evident satisfaction. If there had been an atmosphere of disharmony when first the wedding was announced, it had evaporated since. Everywhere she looked there were smiling faces and happy laughter.

Only one sour note touched the day, and Alessandra was half of a mind that she had imagined it, or misinterpreted it. Two women who she did not recognize, but assumed to be friends of her mother's, introduced themselves as the Ladies Jacqueline and Letitia Bremcott. Upon hearing their names, she knew them at once, for in years past the Bremcotts had been frequent visitors to the Huntingsley estates. Alessandra had played with a then youthful Jacqueline on more than one occasion. "How good to see you again!" she had cried with enthusiasm.

They murmured that they had come to offer her their felicitations. "Such a lovely wedding. Your mother must be proud to have put it together so . . . cleverly," Lady Letitia had said with a small, but weighty, pause.

"Why, thank you," Alessandra had said, her smile failing just a little at the unexpected censure she could not miss. "I shall tell her you approve."

A singular eyebrow rose above Lady Letitia's austere expression, a telling movement, but she offered no further comment.

Lady Jacqueline offered her gloved hand, and even bent to give Alessandra a tiny kiss on the cheek. "You must be good to my dear . . . to Jeffrey. He is the finest fellow, and deserves the very best. But I know you will wish to be a kind-hearted, obedient wife, for his sake." She raised her green eyes and gazed frankly across the room directly at him. She raised a hand with which she gave him a graceful and familiar little wave. He lifted his hand in a gesture of smiling acknowledgement, and for a moment Alessandra felt the urge to also wave at her new husband, though why she should suddenly care so keenly to do so she could not bring herself to imagine.

"I shall do my best," Alessandra said, bringing an unnatural smile to her lips.

Jacqueline responded merely, "Ah, yes."

The two younger women looked at each other steadily. Alessandra saw the delicate figure before her, the rich gown of watered peach silk, the tasteful, subtle inclusion of diamond-studded combs in the curly coiffure that was all the latest rage, the dainty features that formed a more than merely attractive face, and suddenly Alessandra felt she had neglected to ask Jeffrey something quite important, something that it had not occurred to her to ask until this very moment.

The two ladies made their excuses, and then once again Alessandra was pulled into a whirl of congratulations and merrymaking, so that she forgot all about the two ladies, until quite some time later.

Chapter 6

"So, here are the tickets then. *Muy bien*, eh?" Lord Malcolm said, clasping his hands behind his back and rocking on his heels in satisfaction.

"You are speaking Spanish, my dear, not Italian," his wife corrected him. She turned to the newlyweds, and gaily asked, "So what do you think of our little surprise?"

Jeffrey opened his mouth, but had to close it to reconsider what he was going to say. Finally he managed to say, "A trip to Italy. My heavens. That is quite a honeymoon, heh, Alessandra?"

She was not sure what the expression on his face meant, but it stifled a little of the pleasure she had felt when Papa had announced that he was paying for them to honeymoon in Italy.

"Rome. The Acropolis, the Colosseum," she said, trying to sound thrilled. "I think I am the luckiest girl alive." She crossed the room to give both of her parents a hug.

"It is my fault they are not as excited as they would have been, Malcolm, for I am afraid I let the cat out of the bag a little earlier today. I told Lessie she could wear her new dress for her going away, and since our children are naturally bright, I suspect this honeymoon trip did not come as the big surprise we had intended."

"Amelia!" Malcolm scolded mildly, too pleased with the day's work to really be upset.

"Come along, children," Lady Amelia said, of a sudden rising to her feet.

Alessandra all at once realized that her mother was signaling it was time to retire for the night. Jeffrey and she looked at each other quickly, and he rose as well. Alessandra came slowly to her feet, taking her cue from him. Why hadn't they discussed this moment beforehand? What had she envisioned would happen at this time? The truth was that she had not gotten that far in her thoughts. She had thought "I shall talk with Jeffrey to see what he expects of me as his wife" and had allowed that to be the end of the matter in her mind. She hadn't even thought through where they were going to be after the wedding: whose home? One of their own, or with a parent? Would they have separate rooms? Adjoining ones? It had all happened so fast, there wasn't time for whys and wherefores.

She was finding it an easy thing to play the newlywed girl, letting her eyes remain demurely on the carpet at their feet.

"I have another little surprise for you, my dears," Amelia said, crooking a finger at them, which Jeffrey interpreted as meaning they were meant to follow her.

She led them up the stairs, where they encountered

Emmeline, who was just returning from tucking her little brother into bed. He was, of course, too old to require a tucking in bed, but it had been mutually, however silently, agreed that he was also too young to be trusted to not get up to some wedding-night mischief, and he was therefore escorted to his room by his eldest sister.

"Good night," Emmeline said. She gave Alessandra a smile and a knowing nod, which Alessandra tried to act as though she had not seen. On the other hand, she saw quite clearly that Jeffrey gave Emmeline a big, broad wink, one that caused her older sister to blush a becoming shade of pink. Oh, that dratted sense of humor of his! Really, he was doing it too brown.

Instead of going to the left to the family's bed-chambers, Lady Amelia turned to the right. Alessandra frowned to herself, recalling that her father's library was this way, and the little atrium, and the access to the roof, and . . .

"The Sapphire Room," her mother announced proudly, swinging the door open wide.

"Oh, yes," Alessandra said wanly. "The Bridal Room."

"You had forgotten hadn't you, my dear? Well, I had not. And it is so apropos, since you wore Aunt Agatha's sapphires today." She leaned toward Jeffrey to place a hand on his arm and confide, "Every woman for the past two hundred years who has spent her wedding night in New Garden Hall had spent it here. It's a tradition."

"I see," Jeffrey said dryly, blinking several times, his face studiously blank.

"My dear, we are *de trop*," Malcolm said, catching up his wife's hand and draping it over his arm. "Good night

61

all," he called over his shoulder as he led his wife away.

Alessandra went into the room at once, moving through the large proportions of the interior toward the door that indicated another room off the larger one. After a minute's time, she came from the smaller room and announced in a wail that echoed, "No cot. No bedding. Nothing!"

Jeffrey stepped into the room as well, reaching to close the door behind him. "You mean *that*," he asked, lifting a hand and an eyebrow to indicate the carved fourposter bed against the far wall, "is the only sleeping accouterments available in this entire cavernous room?"

"That's exactly what I mean. Oh, Jeffrey, we must go back to them and explain how it is to be. I had thought . . . I don't know . . . that somehow I'd be someplace, and you'd be someplace else . . . and, oh, I don't know! I didn't think, that's the truth of it!"

"Calm yourself, Alessandra. Come, there's a nice fire burning in—my heavens!—all three grates. Though I doubt even three are enough to heat this room, if one can call a cave a room." He smiled at her, and his very calmness helped restore her composure. He was right, her blue sarcenet gown was too thin to allow her to stay long from the source of heat, so she moved to stand directly in front of one of the fireplaces.

"My heavens! Is *everything* in here blue? I confess I had forgotten this monstrous room existed. Whyever does it do so?" he could not help but be distracted enough to ask as he gazed about in a mix of renewed aversion and amazement that had been a part of his long-ago and nearly forgotten past.

"It was built to encourage some monarch or duke or

other to stay here. His colors obviously included sapphire blue. When whoever it was fell out of favor, it became just the 'Sapphire Room," and has been so for so long that no one seems to recall who the famous person was."

"Ah, Cromwell, perhaps? Or good Queen Bess? No, not blue, and, no, she never fell out of favor, at least not to the extent that we should have forgotten her by now."

"Who cares about the room's history, Jeffrey?" Alessandra cried, wrapping her cooling arms around herself.

"Quite right. Back to the business at hand, of course. Please have a seat. I must speak to you before I go to speak with your father."

Her mouth formed a half-crescent frown, indicating her obvious disorientation. The evening was as topsy-turvy in its experiences as the day had been, yet she did as she was bid, and moved to pull one of the heavy sapphire-colored velvet-covered chairs nearer to the fire. There she sat, looking at him half-expectantly and half-puzzled.

"I should have spoken of this before the ceremony today, but there was no time, no occasion to do so. At any rate, the result would be the same: you and I would have still needed to go through with the ceremony." He sat down as well, leaning toward her, his elbows on his knees, his hands loosely clasped before him.

She frowned a little more, but said nothing.

"I have had some rather good advice. You see, by marrying we have scotched all the tawdry rumors and set our reputations to rights once more. However, there is no particular reason for us to . . ." he hesitated, disturbed by something in her expression. Perhaps it was her very youth, that sort of trusting look that only innocents can achieve, or perhaps it was merely a case where delicacy must give way to the awkwardness of honesty, something he found he was loathe to do of a sudden. There was the fact that the offer of an annulment was, however it came to be, even at best faintly insulting to the lady. He shook his head, bringing himself back to the point at hand and proceeded, "Er! . . . that is, that there is no need for us to remain married. I propose that before we set out on any honeymoon, which I assume your father will not care to frank once he sees we do not mean to make a go of it and which, under the circumstances, would be really quite absurd . . . *Ahem!* at any rate, I propose that I immediately file for an annulment."

A harsh, shocked silence fell between them, broken only by the ticking of an ornate ormolu clock over one of the mantelpieces.

"Well? " he said at length, rubbing his hands together as though he were cold or nervous. He peered through the evening's gloom toward her.

"Well," she said in an arid, squeaky voice, and then again, "Well."

The clock ticked some more; in fact, he counted exactly twenty-seven strokes of the second hand before she spoke again. "On what grounds?" she asked.

"Nonconsummation, of course."

"Ah. Of course. I see."

He sat back in the heavy, engulfing chair, feeling the need to squirm, but resisting it. Her voice was nearly devoid of emotion, yet faintly accusatory . . . or was that hurt he heard in her tone?

"I can see that you are right," she said at last. Her features had grown as stoic as her voice.

He released the breath that he had not realized he'd been holding, and came to his feet, ostensibly to move closer to the fire. He made a determined effort not to pace, choosing instead to cross his arms as he spoke brusquely, "Right enough, then. I'll go and speak with your father. He'll see the way of it, I'm sure."

"Will there have to be any kind of settlement?" she asked, aware that her voice sounded flat and lifeless.

"Do you mean monies?" Despite his resolve, he began to pace back and forth in front of the fireplace, wishing she'd let him go to speak with Lord Malcolm, the sooner to find his bed—wherever that might be— this night.

"Yes."

"Well, no. I mean to say, I just assumed that we should each go away from this as we came into it. Does that not seem fair?"

"Quite fair." She looked down at her hands clasped tightly in her lap, the gold and diamond ring winking up at her as though to taunt her for all her worrying, all her fancying how this "marriage" would work out. It was an heirloom from his family; his mother had provided it. "So you will return my dowry to Papa?"

"We never quite got to actually discussing that. But I'll make it quite clear that I have no intention of taking it."

He saw her flinch as though someone had thrown a blow toward her face, and perceived that she could not help but be smarting at least a little that he wanted no part of her, that he so quickly denounced any connection to her, having only just married her.

"You'll see," he said, feeling strangely cruel and wanting to correct that misconception, to himself as well as to her. He moved to place a hand on her shoulder. She turned her face in the opposite direction, her posture correct but stiff. "You will be free to experience your first season, and to find someone to love, or at least more suited to you. 'Twould be a shame to let other people's expectations dictate how we must live the rest of our lives, wouldn't you agree?"

She moved a little, half shrugging his hand from her shoulder, so that he pulled it back and stepped away. "Of course I agree," she said firmly. She rose to her feet, smoothing her skirts with her hands, her chin held high. "Shall we go to see Papa?"

"My dear girl, I think perhaps I should go alone. I suspect this will not be well received."

She glared at him, for a flash thinking to reprimand him for deigning to "protect her sensibilities," but the truth of the matter was that she did not care to enact yet another scene, was not sure she could maintain any semblance of poise. She nodded and returned to her seat, rubbing her arms as if she could not get warm enough.

He moved to the door, then, glancing back at her petite form shivering in the near dark, paused. He returned into the room, the heels of his Hessians clicking over the marble floor. He went to the bed, and pulled off the huge quilted comforter and carried it back to her.

"Here, Alessandra. Wrap up in this."

"No, thank you. I believe . . . I am just going to return to my own room."

He drew back the offering hand and let the comforter

slip to the floor. He made a clipped bow, accompanied by a military turn, and said as he moved away, "Until we meet tomorrow."

As soon as he was gone she fled her seat, flying down the hall to her old room, her eyes dry but her throat locked against the wail that threatened to erupt past her closely held composure.

Chapter 7

"What's the matter with my Lessie!" Lord Malcolm demanded to know, his voice unnaturally deep as his fist crashed down on the lowboy in his sitting room, the bibelots that littered its top dancing nervously. Lord Malcolm's floor-length robe had begun to come untied, exposing the white nightshirt underneath, and his night-cap had already fallen forgotten to the floor, exposing his graying head to the night's chill.

"My dear, please, calm yourself before you have an attack of apoplexy!" Lady Amelia pleaded, her hands clasped tightly before her, her hastily thrown-on peignoir slightly askew.

"It is not a matter of anything being amiss with your daughter, sir," Jeffrey said, his face as tight as his voice.

"Then why in Hades is there all this talk of an annulment, I ask you?"

"Please, Malcolm, your voice! Think of the servants."

"Sir, I explained that this was merely a way for Alessandra and I to go on with our lives—" Jeffrey said quietly.

"Why can't you go on with them together?!" Lord Malcolm hissed in a stage whisper in a vain attempt to accede to his wife's behest.

"You know that this was no love match, sir."

"Well then, demmit, *make* it one!"

"Such language!" Amelia cried, hiding her distress behind censure.

"Really, Lord Malcolm. I cannot imagine you are thinking this situation all the way through. I have saved your daughter's reputation—"

"Only to ruin it! Why? Why!" The older man leaned toward the younger, his fists becoming clenched at his sides, his eye trained on the fellow before him, demanding an answer.

"In what possible way will it be ruined?" Jeffrey asked warmly, allowing a shade of his growing impatience to show.

"You mean to leave the girl on her wedding night, and you ask me 'What possible way?'" Lord Malcolm cried, throwing his arms up in the air in a gesture of disbelief. "Do you think servants don't talk? Do you think it won't be whispered about that Alessandra Hamilton was such a quiz that her husband would not even spend one night with her? Bah!" he cried, suddenly throwing himself into one of his wife's sitting-room chairs, his hands holding either side of his head.

"I don't mean to insult her. Nor you, sir," Jeffrey said sincerely.

Lord Malcolm looked up at last, hearing the honesty in the younger man's words, seeing that the lad thought he was doing what was right.

His face scrunched into a mask of thoughtfulness and exasperation combined, and he leaned forward to plant his hands on his knees, his elbows at right angles, obviously assessing the situation, trying to control his anger.

"What does Lessie say to all this? You have spoken to her, I should hope?" he demanded.

"I have. She is agreed."

Lady Amelia uttered some sort of prayer or invocation, and sank into the chair next to her husband's.

Lord Malcolm fell silent, his mouth held tightly closed as he stared at the man before him. At length, he sighed, and stood once again. He planted himself before Jeffrey, his arms crossed in resignation. "All right. All right!" he sighed heavily. "It could be worse, I suppose."

He gave his wife an incomprehensible look when she moaned and slumped back in her chair, then turned to Jeffrey and said, "I'll sign any annulment papers laid before me, but only if I have your promise in one thing."

"My lord?"

"An annulment can go forth on the grounds of non-consummation so long as we all know that to be true. We can be as discreet as we like about the whole demme thing. I've an uncle who's a bishop. I'll talk to him. He'll help us.

"Until such time, however, I'll not have Alessandra subjected to humiliation. I want you to promise me this one thing. If you won't, then I won't sign the annulment papers, and with Alessandra being under the age of her majority, it'll be three years before you can get her to sign 'em for herself."

Again Jeffrey indicated he was listening by saying, "Sir?"

"I want you to promise me that you'll stay here in this house with her, share the Sapphire Room with her, until the annulment comes through." He hurried on, "I

71

don't care where you sleep in that room, be it on the floor or in the wardrobe, just so long as you give the servants no cause to talk about it. No extra bedding or cots. And you'll have to straighten up after yourself; make it look normal like."

Jeffrey met Lord Malcolm's gaze steadily, stunned. He stared for a moment, only to then smile faintly, comprehension dawning. "It won't happen as you think," he said slowly.

Lady Amelia sat up and looked at the two men, her eyes darting about as she cried, "But if they share a room . . . ! Then the servants would have to attest that the two spent their nights together. What of any annulment then?"

Lord Malcolm's eyes narrowed but did not waver from Jeffrey's. He said curtly, "I just don't want m'girl humiliated."

"You think—you hope—that nature will take its course?" Jeffrey almost laughed, a little in awe of his temporary father-in-law's cunning. He continued, "You must know that I have my own connections with the Church. I see no reason why the servants need ever be asked to attest to anything. As you say, these things can be done discreetly."

"So you have no reason to object to my one condition. And the point of the matter is, I'll not sign any papers unless you promise me this."

Jeffrey became aware of a kind of grudging admiration for Lord Malcolm, knowing he had met a strategist, one that would not back away from his position.

There was nothing for it. "Very well, sir. I agree," he said.

Lord Malcolm "hmphed" and stuck out his hand, which Jeffrey took and shook. Then he said to Jeffrey,

"You are, I know, a man of your word."

"I am. As are you," Jeffrey said, and smiled after the manner of a man who sees himself as the victor.

Lord Malcolm laughed himself then also, gruffly, at the boy's cheekiness. "She's pretty, my Lessie," he said, not bothering to hide his feelings or anticipations.

"She is."

"And you like her."

"I do, yes."

"And you'll share the Sapphire Room with her?"

"If she'll allow it."

"She will, I'll see to that. And you truly mean to stay away from the girl, and annul the marriage?"

"I do."

Lord Malcolm grinned again, in a manner very like that Jeffrey had just done, then sighed, and turned to offer his wife a hand up to her feet. She looked from one to the other, not quite sure how things had been resolved.

"Madam," Jeffrey addressed her, "I believe you will find that Alessandra has returned to her former room."

"Oh, the dear girl. I'll go and explain why she must return to the Sapphire Room . . . ?" Lady Amelia looked to her husband with narrowed eyes; it was clear that she was not sure that her daughter could share a room with a man *and* still have an annulment as well.

"Amelia! You go on back to bed. *I'll* speak with Alessandra and see that she understands," Malcolm ordered.

"Oh, Malcolm. Do see that you are not too abrupt with her!" Lady Amelia beseeched him, even as she moved to return to the inner room which was their bedchamber.

"Alessandra will understand," Lord Malcolm assured the younger man, as he signaled with a wave of his hand that they should proceed on their separate ways.

"As to that," Jeffrey said with a slow smile that was not entirely artificial, "I am glad it falls to you to explain it all to her." He bowed to his father-in-law and left him.

Returned to the Sapphire Room, which he suspected would each time he entered strike him anew as being dark and overwhelming with its collection of articles and furnishings almost exclusively in blue shades, Jeffrey went through several chests of drawers until he found the one that had his clothing neatly arranged within it. He removed his cravat, his watch and fob, and his money purse and set them on the blue velvet-covered dresser top. He then went to both wardrobes, the second of which contained the few coats, jackets, and neatly and freshly pressed inexpressibles he had had sent ahead of him to New Garden Hall. He smiled mildly to himself as he looked at them, thinking that Lord Malcolm's servants were certainly efficient, and almost without doubt, as wont to gossip as Lord Malcolm feared.

He pulled the comforter he had earlier offered to Alessandra from off the floor and wrapped it about his body, then sat before the fire. It was a demme chilly room, even for June, he thought. He stared into the flames, willing his mind to rest and think of nothing, but before long he was bored and wishing that he had something to read. That thought led to the fact that there was only one lamp lighted, and that surely such a gargantuan room must have more than one lamp.

He rose, doffed his blanket with a disapproving shiver, and moved about the room until he had located and collected six lamps. Old lectures from his nanny came to mind to assure him that it was a decidedly wasteful thing to light them all, but Jeffrey proceeded to do so, thinking Lord Malcolm could safely absorb the expense, the least the man could do for all the trouble he, Jeffrey, was being put to.

He picked up one of the lamps and circled the room, looking into cupboards and drawers and on to shelves. In no time he had located some books, all dry travel and exploration tomes, but there was one about America which at least promised to have some interesting tales of savages hidden among its pages.

He took it back to his chair, wrapped himself again in the coverlet, and opened the book so that the assorted lights fell upon it to best advantage.

He was starting to feel a little drowsy when the door opened quietly and Alessandra stepped in. Her hair was no longer pinned up on her head, but caught back in a long, dark braid. She kept her eyes down, her expression grim, and she stopped only two steps into the room. For a moment he recalled the same expression upon the face of a five year old, that time he had roundly scolded her for finking on him to his father. He had made the bad mistake of trying to get his father's miniature ship most unsuccessfully out of its bottle, and she had had the bad grace to report it.

"Come to the fire," he said gently, for it was obvious she was fighting back tears. He did not ask her if her father had explained; that was self-evident by her very presence in the room.

She did not move for a moment, but finally she stepped forward woodenly and sat stiffly on the edge of the chair opposite his own, blinking until her misty eyes no longer threatened to overflow.

"If my father meant to save me from humiliation, he

would not have made me do this," she said in ringing tones, staring straight ahead, her lower lip trembling.

"You understand what he is doing." He said it as a statement rather than a question.

"Yes."

"Then let us make the best of it, shall we? I'm hungry. Are you? Shall I ring for something to eat?"

She darted a look at him, and slowly sank back into her chair. "All right," she agreed, her lower lip retreating a little. "And I would like some chocolate."

"Sounds enchanting. I myself have had enough champagne for one day." So saying, he rose, still wrapped in his bulky covering, and waddled to the bellpull by the bed. After he had tugged the braided cord, trusting that it would ring somewhere belowstairs for it certainly did not make a sound in the room, he waddled back to his chair, dragging a second blanket from off the bed behind him. "My dear?" he offered it to Alessandra.

She accepted the offering and stood to wrap it around herself, unable to keep a sigh of appreciation from passing her lips as she snuggled down once again into the chair. He noted that the chair was large enough that her toes scarcely touched the carpet when she sat back.

A servant soon appeared, and if Patty was surprised to find the couple wrapped in blankets, surrounded by a half circle of lighted lamps, Alessandra far outside her husband's reach, asking that an array of foodstuffs be delivered to their room, she did not let it show.

She came back with a heavy tray that she had almost had to ask Angie to help carry up, the chocolate steaming in its pot next to a wide array of taste tempters the cook had lovingly prepared for the newlyweds. That they were hungry was not so surprising, but Patty did blink when

76

she was asked to bring a deck of cards. Between the newlyweds sat a small table upon which resided a cribbage board, having been located on the top shelf of one of the wardrobes, its pegs already placed in the starting positions in anticipation of a game.

When Patty returned with the deck of cards, she made her curtsy to each of them after being assured they required nothing else, and said, "The whole staff sends their best wishes on this happy day, Lady Huntingsley, Lord Huntingsley."

Jeffrey and Alessandra looked at each other in something very like astonishment, but then Alessandra inclined her head graciously and thanked the woman. As Patty pulled the door to behind herself, the servant smiled a little at the newlywed jitters that caused the young couple to delay the evening with games and supper.

"So, you have a new name," Jeffrey teased lightly as he reached around the folds of his comforter for the deck of cards.

"I suppose I do. For now. 'Lady Huntingsley,'" she parroted, the name so strange and alien to her ears.

She watched him shuffle, the cards blending evenly and with measure, quite unlike her own disjointed thoughts. Her comment that she had his name, for now, might have been bitterly said, but some of the sting had begun to go out of the evening already, now that she had had time to realign her thinking, now that she had seen how Jeffrey seemed so calm. She should not have been so upset by his pronouncement. She should not have let Emmeline and Mama's little chats influence her into thinking this marriage had any semblance of normality about it. She should not think of his choice to end their alliance as being in any way unkind. The truth must surely be self-evident: he wasn't trying to reject *her* per se, he was actually rejecting marriage. He was being clear-headed, where she had not. Yes, it was really rather a kindness that he sought to give her, this other chance at a later, more planned, perhaps more congenial attachment to someone of her own choosing.

He was treating her as decently as he could, given their peculiar set of circumstances, she told herself. The very least she could do was to cooperate and be as decent in return.

If she heard the tiny sound, the sad little tolling of a death knell for the passing of a dream, she could only scold herself for having dared to give it even a moment of life, even a hint of existence in her imagination.

"I . . . I'm sorry if I made a fuss earlier," she ventured to say, reaching to pick up the cards as he dealt them to her.

"We all made fusses today. I think it goes with weddings. And annulments, of course."

She was proud of herself for not wincing this time when he said that word. "Exactly so, I should say," she said, trying to match his matter-of-fact demeanor.

"Exactly so."

She selected two cards and placed them in the crib, on his side of the table, frowning at the cards left in her hand. "I should very much like to see an eight turned up." She hoped her voice carried the right inflection, that it said she might as well be at a card party as sitting here with a man who had married her, yet declined to be her husband.

When he had added two of his cards to the crib, she

reached to cut the deck, and he turned over a jack.

"His nibs," he said, and moved his peg.

"Drat."

"Such language! I can't have that from my wife, you know," he cried in mock offense, one hand at his breast as though in outrage.

For a moment he thought his playful endeavor had crossed the line of humor into bad taste, but then she actually smiled at him.

"Then I shall make an effort to be very careful of my tongue—for a few weeks, at least."

He smiled back. "At the end of which you may be your own self once more."

"My own self," she said, still smiling for his benefit, even while a little voice inside her head asked, *And who exactly is "my own self" now? How will this odd venture in and out of marriage change me? Will I ever be the same as once I was?*

The ring on her finger flashed in the lamp light, making her long to take it off.

In time, she told herself, in time.

When Jeffrey had won the sixth game to her fifth, they set the cards aside. They had eaten as much as they cared for of the large meal, both when first it was warm, and later when it had grown cold. They had drunk all the chocolate, and decided against ringing for tea. They had talked about their respective childhoods, recalling mutual occasions when the families had come together, and had finally deduced that they were related to one another through a second marriage of a great-aunt.

Jeffrey, his eyes heavy, looked to the ormolu clock ticking above their heads. "It's four in the morning!" he cried.

"Really?" Alessandra asked, stifling a yawn behind her hand. "I had no idea."

They sat in silence for a while, until Jeffrey stood. "Come, help me push these chairs together."

She saw his intention, and rose with her lips arranged in a straight line, making no comment. After a little trouble with the rug, they finally managed to push the chairs together to form a short bed. "It's way too short," she said, shaking her head. "Even for me."

"I am afraid I must admit that to sleep thusly would surely cripple me, a fate I shouldn't mind avoiding. Hmmm. Well then," he said, stroking his chin as he considered the problem. "If only we could put our hands on some extra bedding, I'd simply make a sort of pallet here on the rug. I could pretend I was sleeping in the woods, as Father and Elias and I used to do for sport," he said lightly, making her look at him with appreciation that he knew how to make light of an awkward situation.

She moved to the bed and pulled at the coverings. "There are two blankets more here, beside the comforter you have there and the blanket that I had, plus the sheets. You could have those two, I suppose? Be sure you take the comforter, it's heavier. You'll need it; the floor beneath the rugs is marble. I'll retain these two blankets and the sheets, as the sheets couldn't add overmuch to your comfort, I'm assured."

"All right then," he said, but his tone was not overly eager.

He made a narrow bedding on the floor, opposite the

bed, by folding the comforter in thirds and laying it on the rug. She tossed him two of the four pillows that were on the bed, which he arranged on top of the comforter, and over which he spread the remaining blanket.

He crossed to the chest where he knew his clothes were stored, and after opening three drawers found the one where his nightshirts had been placed. He turned to her, gave an eloquent half-shrug, then said "I'll change in the adjoining room."

When he had gone into the little dressing room and shut the door, Alessandra flew to the chests of drawers, hurriedly opening drawers until she found her own night garments. The first one that came to hand was a serviceable old flannel gown. She ran across the room, and threw open a door of each of the two opposing wardrobes, forming a smallish but protective triangle in the center of which she quickly shrugged out of her clothes, thinking that if he returned soon, she would be at least in part sheltered from view. She cursed silently at some of the small buttons in the back of her gown, but managed to get enough undone that she could slip the garment off even though she could not unfasten them all. She hesitated over her petticoats for a moment, but decided they would be terribly uncomfortable to sleep in. The simple fact that she would feel rather exposed, despite the hardiness of her nightgown, was something she would have to ignore. If this whole annulment process was going to take weeks, or—heaven forbid!—months, she could not give up her nights' rest for that entire time. Better to start off right, she supposed with a sigh.

He knocked before coming back into the room.

"Come in," she called, sitting already safely ensconced

in the bed in her nightcap, with the covers pulled up around her chin.

"I forgot my robe," he said a little sheepishly. He carried his clothing before him, as if he could hide the nightshirt he wore behind the various articles of clothing that dangled over his arm. He still wore his stockings, evidently having neglected to find his slippers as well.

"You might check to see if it's in the wardrobe," she suggested helpfully, daring to allow a hand out from under the covers to point in the general direction.

"Yes, probably." He crossed to the wardrobe and did not see it, so he reached to part some of the articles hanging there to search for it. His clothes still dangled from under his arm until he reached up, and then some of the pieces fell onto the floor. With a big sigh, he stooped and retrieved them, then with a shrug threw them all onto the floor of the wardrobe. "My man Winters will be arriving tomorrow. After he dressed me this morning, I gave him the day off," he said apologetically as he closed the wardrobe door.

"Fine," she said, suddenly wanting to giggle. She had never seen a man in a nightshirt before, not even her father. One must discount Oliver, who, at nearly six years her junior, was hardly a manly example.

Jeffrey looked rather boyish in his, especially as the awkwardness of the moment lent a touch of color to his prominent cheekbones.

"Good night," she said, snuggling down into the covers so that he could not see her foolishly grinning.

"Good night."

He rearranged his bedding to suit himself, silently cursing Lord Malcolm and himself both for fools as he blew out the lamps.

He lay down . . .

. . . and lay awake, thinking whirling thoughts that broached all manner of questions that he never came close to answering. It was not long before he began to shiver from the room's incessant and invasive chilliness.

He got up once, to stoke the nearest fire, and lingered there long enough to feel a trifle warmed before heading back to the unwarmed bedding.

After lying there for just a minute, he had a second thought, and decided to pull the bedding closer to the stoked fire, even though it meant moving off the edge of the rug onto the bare floor. This was followed by the logical thought that he should really, since he was up, build up the other fires as well. After a half an hour he had all three fireplaces blazing, and when he laid down before the one, the front side of his body was nearly toasted. He noticed after a short while, however, the side next to the arctic marble floor and his backside were decidedly *not* at all warmed.

He turned over and warmed the backside of his body.

When, one half threatening to shiver, the other perspiring, he turned over yet again, only to feel the sting of the fire's heat caressing a nose that had turned pink from the chill in the air. To add injury to insult, a log snapped and a spark shot out and hit him in the neck. He frantically brushed the ember away, no longer bothering to curse silently.

There was a stirring sound from the bed, but that was all.

After thoroughly inspecting his bedding to make sure he was not going to try to sleep in a smoldering firetrap, he still found he could not sleep.

Ten long minutes later he rose once again, sighing heavily, to attend again the dying fires.

A small voice called out, "Jeffrey?"

"Yes?" he answered, stabbing at the fire with the poker in a decidedly irritable manner.

"Is it any warmer there by the fire? I am freezing to death."

He hung his head for a moment and half-laughed to himself. "No," he called back churlishly.

"Oh."

He turned toward her, unaware that he was back-lighted by the fires and that he was presenting an outline of his form beneath his nightshirt. "Listen," he said. "There's nothing for it, and I think your wily old father knows it. He would have spent a wedding night in this drafty monstrosity of a room himself, I should dare to claim. He's made sure that we're going to *have* to share a bed, this bed, and in that way, therefore, the covers."

She was silent for a moment, during which he wondered if she was really going to choose to let him freeze to death, or at least chill so badly as to have a terrible cold for the rest of their abbreviated marriage. Her eyes, through the gloom of the half-light before dawn, were very wide as she peered out of the bed toward him.

"Well . . . yes. I can see that we are in a bad spot here," she finally said hesitantly.

"We'll just take two of these pillows and place them between us. We are above our animal selves, or so the preachers have always told me. I see no reason why we must freeze to death to remain . . . separate."

"Of course we need not," Alessandra agreed quickly, breathlessly, at last averting her eyes. What had she seen, anyway? Nothing. Merely his outline. So why did she feel as if someone had hit her in the stomach with a brick?

Jeffrey brought the bedding items back to the bed and spread them out, tossing the pillows to Alessandra to arrange. When she scooted from the middle of the bed onto unwarmed sheets, she gritted her teeth against the renewed chill as she arranged the two pillows, which she could not seem to quite fluff up to her satisfaction, down the middle of the bed. She lay back, burrowing under the covers, only her dark-haired head with the little night-cap tied under her chin showing.

"I should have thought to wonder why the servants did not leave the warming pans for the sheets. I cannot imagine why they did not," she said through teeth that threatened to chatter.

"I can. Your father's orders, no doubt," Jeffrey grumbled as he drew back the covers on his side and slid under.

Alessandra had not shared a bed in many a year, and then of course only with her sister or her girlfriends. She knew her senses were heightened, but still it seemed his weight made the mattress slant toward the middle quite a bit. She found herself wondering how many couples had spent a wedding night on this very mattress, and how many of them had shared the spot in the middle, leaving this troublesome dip that she found herself sliding toward.

"Dash it all!" she heard Jeffrey mutter from the other side of the pillows, quite possibly discovering the mattress's condition for himself. She grinned to herself crookedly, for the night had been very strange and growing more so, disintegrating into the realm of the absurd. She tried to find a position that allowed her to hold on to the side of the mattress.

"Good night," she said quietly once she thought she had achieved her goal.

"Good *morning*," he said with emphasis.

Before very long, warmer at last, they were both sound asleep.

Chapter 8

Jeffrey was gone by the time she awakened. She was near to the center of the bed, the pillows running a line along her spine. She looked around the room and saw that a drawer was open about an inch, and Jeffrey's watch and money purse were gone, so she knew he had dressed already.

She pushed back the covers reluctantly, and hurried to the wardrobe to locate her robe and slippers. Pulling them on, she went to the dressing room, just to double-check that she was indeed alone in the room.

Seeing that to be true, she went back to the bed and climbed under the covers, still wearing her robe and slippers, and reached for the bellpull.

She started to lean back, to soak up a few more minutes of warmth and quiet, but then she sat up again abruptly, reaching for the two pillows that ran down the middle of the bed, throwing them haphazardly toward the head of the bed. She tried to tell herself that she was setting the bed to rights to help Jeffrey keep his bargain with her father, but in truth she did it, even as her father had predicted, so that she would not be embarrassed in front of the servants.

Patty responded within a few minutes, bringing a loaded tray with her.

"Tea!" Alessandra breathed, as if the woman had brought her nectar.

"Lord love us, Miss Les . . . I mean, my lady, it's right nippy in here!" Patty cried as she set the breakfast tray on its sturdy legs in front of her mistress. "Shall I see to the fires?"

Alessandra nodded vigorously, her mouth already full of warm muffins as she poured the steaming tea into a delicate cup. She proceeded on to the fried eggs and ham as if she had not eaten in days. A glance at the clock arrested her efforts for a moment, and she cried in a muffled voice, "Never say 'tis two in the afternoon!"

"'Tis," the maid said simply, beaming at her lady from where she poked at the fire. Patty plainly thought she knew the reason why her ladyship had slept so late.

At the knowing look a little of Alessandra's ravenous appetite dissipated, but she helped herself to a second cup of tea. "Is . . . is Lord Huntingsley still to home, or has he gone out?" she asked, wondering if she sounded properly informed. Did wives always know where their husbands were, or what their plans were? One would have to say that was largely true of Mama and Papa, but she was not sure they were a standard against which others should be measured.

"He's gone out, my lady."

"Ah. Well, he said he might," she fibbed.

Patty nodded cheerily, and said, "He won't be gone long, I reckon." And she actually giggled.

Alessandra set her cup down with a rattle. This

charade of a marriage was going to be quite an exercise in the ludicrous, she could see that right now.

"I'd like to get dressed," she said, pushing the tray away. "I must speak with Papa."

"He's to home. Just come back, and in a good mood, too." Patty had taken it as her right to speak her mind for some time now, for she had been with the Hamiltons for over twenty years.

"I am happy to hear that," Alessandra said with feeling, even as she wondered what reason her father might have to be in a good mood. Lord Malcolm did not like scenes, and he had been presented with any number of them lately, the last—and worst—being just last night. Yes, she definitely needed to talk to him, she thought as she began to get dressed.

"Alessandra!" her father greeted her fondly as she came into his study. One hand was on a ledger, holding its pages open, the other was scribbling away at a worksheet. "How may I help you?"

She scowled at him, for he was decidedly altogether too cheery. She sat in the chair placed before his desk, her arms crossed and settled on the desktop before her as she watched the columns of numbers grow in neat lines. A glance told her it had something to do with the shipping interests the family quietly supported, the old and revered source of their revenue beyond their farming interests. In fact, they had proved such a reliable and valuable source of income that Lord Malcolm did not even leave the accounting to his steward as he did with the farming records. He may not have been as clever a fellow with the accounting books as was recently entitled

Lord Earl Richard Chenmarth—who had received his earldom three years hence in recompense for a somewhat nebulously defined accounting service rendered to poor mad King George just prior to Prinny being made Regent—but neither was he far behind.

"I have come to ask you if you have gone to see Great-Uncle Bartholomew yet," Alessandra asked when it became clear he did not mean to leave off at his endeavors.

"This very morning," he replied, and proceeded to gaily whistle a bit of Beethoven's *Ode to Joy*.

"You told him about the annulment?" She overrode his musical gambit.

"I did."

"And what did he tell you?"

"Oh, he's got to put all the papers together and then present it to the Archbishop." He glanced up at his daughter without moving his head, his eyes immediately going back to his work as his pen flew uninterrupted by her presence or their conversation. "The Archbishop is a busy man, very busy. Could take days to see him. Could take months to have the annulment proceedings in place."

"Papa! You didn't bribe him to slow down the process, did you?" she accused, coming out of her chair.

"I did not."

"Well," she said, drawing back contritely, "I beg your pardon."

"Given, given," he said with a quick, dismissive wave of the hand that did not hold his quill.

As she left the room, he looked up from under his brows and muttered to himself, "He wouldn't *accept* a bribe, drat the man! But at least in the end he was willing

90

to listen to reason, for the sake of the family."

Jacqueline had on her new golden habit, the one she had ordered made from the lovely velvet that so perfectly accented the golden highlights in her hair. She knew the black braid and epaulets were all the crack, and that the black feather that curled from her little military-styled bonnet lent itself well to a contrast with her creamy complexion. She felt very fetching in the new habit and bonnet, and she knew she was turning heads as she rode by.

She spotted any number of acquaintances, and often stopped to chat gaily. The marchioness of Laruche hailed her, so she worked her horse over to the coach which contained the marchioness and her husband.

"You are looking in fine spirits today, my dear," the marchioness told her.

"You are most kind, ma'am."

"When I saw you at that Huntingsley wedding yesterday I thought you were sickening for something."

Jacqueline flushed a deep red. "Did you?"

"You were pale as a ghost. Of course, Laruche here said that was because you were losing out on Chenmarth's boy, that you were miffed to see you weren't to be his countess when the earldom comes his way some day."

"Been an understanding for ages," the marquess mumbled, not bothering to look at either of the ladies rather as though he were conducting an argument with himself.

Jacqueline stared down at him, struggling to keep the horror from her face that his words inspired. Finally she found her voice. "That ancient rumor!" she trilled.

"Doesn't make any difference now he's married, does it, my girl?" the marchioness went on. "You are to tell your mother I sent my greetings, and ask her to call on me about that charity basket we do every fall, won't you? There's a good girl." So saying, she poked her driver with the point of her parasol and they drove on.

Jacqueline sat still long enough that her horse began to grow restless beneath her. Merciful heavens, was the entire Bon Ton talking about her as if she had been left on the shelf? As if Jeffrey Huntingsley had married that girl for any other reason than to correct a social faux pas? Her hands tightened automatically on the reins of her animal, holding him back until her cheeks could begin to cool a little. The groom that rode with her scratched his chin and waited on her pleasure, having missed her humiliation entirely in the sheer boredom of riding at the sedate pace inflicted on him by the park's unwritten rules of conduct.

At length, she focused her attention on those around her. If her behavior had seemed peculiar, no one appeared to have noticed, not even the groom. She spotted the Viscount Aldegard riding his chestnut up an adjoining path. Tilting her chin up with a show of bravado, she urged her horse forward, intercepting him neatly. "My lord," she hailed him. Here, at least, was one who admired her. The groom followed at a languid pace.

The viscount turned toward her call, a smile at the ready, but as soon as he recognized her his face lost any sign of pleasure. "Madam," he said stiffly.

"What brings you to the park on this fine day?" she said at her most coquettish.

It had been her intention to charm him, but his face

grew more frosty, if anything.

"The very fact that it is a fine day," he said with a sniff. "Pardon me. I must hurry to a prior engagement." He did not even wait for her response, but spurred his horse forward in the opposite direction.

She nearly gasped aloud. She had never been snubbed before in her life, and she could not like it. The one man she had thought could never treat her so unkindly had done just that.

How had her life so suddenly changed? She had thought she had the viscount firmly wrapped around her little finger, had thought he absolutely adored her. He had been all that was flattering since her come-out last season, having asked for her hand not even two months after her first appearance. He had gotten her mother's permission, but Jacqueline had never given him an answer. He had offered for her again not yet two weeks ago, having declared his infatuation with her while they had been dancing at Almack's. In fact, she had needed to softly rebuke his ardor that day, turning to flirt with Jeffrey Huntingsley until the Viscount Peter Aldegard could only know his hopes were misplaced. Yet he had lingered at her side, casting wounded, puppy-love eyes her way, making it the most obvious and easiest thing in the world to then turn the tables and flirt with him once more, her new intention now being to make Jeffrey jealous. It was possible, she now reflected, that the subterfuge may not have worked as sweetly as she had thought it ought, especially now she recalled that Lord Aldegard had left in a sudden huff when she had asked to sit out the second dance he had written onto her card, and meanwhile Jeffrey had wandered off to play whist.

Suddenly a light dawned: *that* was why the viscount

was spurning her now. He was jealous! That strong emotion she had hoped to engender in Jeffrey's breast had gone to the other fellow! Of course. This new rejection was only a symptom of his deeper regard.

She sighed with relief, for this made sense of her world once again. The viscount fled from her because he was jealously angry. Jeffrey had married another because he had had no choice. She, Jacqueline, had not lost some vital ingredient, some magic that made her so well sought out and pursued by the opposite gender. No, it was hurt feelings and circumstances that had changed, temporarily, the status quo.

But she could put all to rights again, now that she understood. She would bring the Viscount Aldegard back to heel, to partner her about while she waited to become Jeffrey's bride.

She smiled slowly, and urged her horse forward, nodding to her acquaintances. She was content with the world once more, exchanging gossip and quips, the banter that came so easily to her well-shaped lips inspired by the admiration in the eyes of the gentlemen that hailed her, unable to resist the confident air that only added to her beauty.

Alessandra saw Jeffrey ride into the stableyard from the window of her old room. She had gone there to gather a few belongings to make her stay in the Sapphire Room more congenial, and just happened to be gazing out her window when he rode up.

Her first instinct was to run down and ask him where he had been, for she suspected that, like her father, on this first day of their married life he had been to see a man

94

of the church. Her second instinct told her to stop being a ninny, and to wait until he came to find her. She had a third, much more pressing instinct, one that told her to panic.

How was a soon-to-be-annulled wife supposed to behave? How much of his time should she dare to ask him for? How much time were they expected to spend together? Would they both take their meals at the same table? Should they? If last night was a good example, then she was quite sure they would find they had far too much time together—so maybe she should make an effort to avoid him during the day?

She was so distracted and confused, that she ended up by remaining at her window, staring down into the stable-yard. She saw him come out of the stables and cross the yard. His long muscular legs mounted the steps easily to reach the front doors in but a few moments. He hesitated there and started to raise his hand as if he would reach for the knocker, only to stop in mid-reach. A moment passed, and then he lifted the knocker and released it once, and reached for the door handle to let himself in. Poor fellow! He did not even know if he had the freedom to enter the house without knocking first! Had he truly intended to stay her husband there would have been no question of it.

She moved from the window, cataloging into the back of her mind a comment about his free use of the house, to be presented to him perhaps tonight. That would surely be a good time to talk about these awkward little difficulties they must work around, when no one else was around to see or hear, especially the servants.

He did not come up the stairs looking for her, as she had half-hoped he might and half-feared he would, so she returned to her task of gathering combs, brushes, and other toiletries to move to the Sapphire Room.

When a knock came on her door, she whirled about, dropping several ribbons and hairpins from suddenly inept fingers. "Come in," she breathed, leaning back against the footboard of her old bed for support.

"We have a difficulty," her mother announced, striding into the room with a large box in her arms.

"Oh. Mama," she said, not unaware of the disappointment in her own voice.

"I am afraid that wedding gifts have started to arrive."

"Oh no!" Alessandra cried. "I never thought about gifts!" She came away from the bed, no longer needing its support.

"If I had known that rapscallion Jeffrey was going to pull this terrible annulment business, I should have put on the invitations 'no gifts, please.' But of course that is just crying over spilt milk now, and would have been impossible at any roads."

Emmeline followed her mother's wake into the room, her face, so alike in coloring, if a little more round than her little sister's, was today only a little green around the edges due to morning sickness. "What is this?" she asked, pointing to the box on the bed.

"A wedding gift. From the duchess of Briarcrest, no less," her mother answered sullenly.

"Her grace, The Dragon Duchess of Duke Street?" Emmeline cried, her eyes sparkling. "Lessie, my love, you have come up in the world if you merit a gift from such a lofty one as that. Let's have a look at it, why don't we?" Emmeline's pallor had brightened a little as she beamed at them both.

Mother and daughter exchanged dismayed looks. "We

haven't told Emmeline," Lady Amelia said heavily to Alessandra.

"Told me what?" Emmeline asked, her eyes flying from one unhappy face to the other.

"Lord Huntingsley," Alessandra began, unable to call him by his first name, not under these circumstances, not to her sister's suddenly scowling countenance, "is seeking an annulment."

"What?!" Emmeline cried, her hand flying to her throat in disbelieving astonishment. "But you've only been married one day!"

"I know."

"But why? What possible reason could he have? Did he hide something from us, some disability? Does he have insanity in his family?" she cried, still looking from face to face, and receiving only grimly set mouths as answers. "But why?" she wailed again.

"Emmeline, you must calm down. Remember about the. . . ." Alessandra made a series of little movements with her head as if to urge her to make the logical conclusion to that sentence herself. She did not want to break her promise about keeping Emmeline's pregnancy a secret; it was up to Emmeline to reveal such an important matter herself.

"I'll calm down only when one of you can explain this to me!" Emmeline cried.

"What is Emmeline supposed to be remembering?" Lady Amelia asked slowly, her eyes narrowing.

"You know why Huntingsley and I had to get married. But there really is no reason why we must stay married, so, you see, we are getting this annulment—"

"I asked you a question, both of you. What is it that I don't know about here?" Lady Amelia overrode her daughter's recital.

"But . . . but . . . that's *dishonorable!*" Emmeline cried, ignoring her mother.

"It is not. I have agreed. How can you say that? Jeffrey is—"

"Emmeline! Alessandra!" Lady Amelia clapped her hands together in impatience.

"Oh, Mama," Alessandra cried, exasperated beyond the end of her endurance. "Why don't you just hush up!"

Silence fell like a blow, interrupted only by Lady Amelia's rapid breathing and fanning of the air in front of her utterly astonished expression.

Alessandra covered her mouth with both hands, choked back a sob, and ran from the room.

"Well, I never! That girl will have to be punished," Lady Amelia said in a faint voice.

Emmeline stared at the doorway through which her sister had just disappeared from the room. "Perhaps she already has been," she said quietly.

"So what is this secret you girls are keeping from me?"

Reaching absently to twirl a lock of hair around her finger in worried agitation, Emmeline said, "Oh, Mama, hush up."

Chapter 9

"I have some wonderful news to impart to you all," Lady Amelia said, her eyes dancing as she stood at her end of the dining table, her hands lightly clasped in front of her.

Malcolm looked up from his meal, wondering if she meant to tell them that Jeffrey's valet Walters . . . no, Winters . . . had arrived this afternoon. It was the bane of his existence, this need of Amelia's to tell all the household tidbits throughout the dinnertime. He suspected these sorts of announcements were largely due to the fact that she forgot things she ought to know unless she spoke them aloud.

"Our Emmeline is increasing," Amelia said with a happy grin.

"Increasing what?" Oliver asked through the pudding he had just spooned into his mouth.

"She's going to have a baby, nodcock," Lord Malcolm explained to his son, his face breaking into a wreath of smiles at the unexpected news. "My first grandchild!" he stated happily. However, the smile instantly faded as he demanded, "So where is James? What was he thinking, allowing you to travel alone at such a time?"

"Oh, Papa, don't be so old-fashioned. The doctor said I might come, as long as I used our private carriage, because it is so well sprung, you know," Emmeline chided him good-naturedly. "And as you very well know, James has had to go to the Consulate in Brussels. There was nothing for it, so I was very pleased indeed to receive Mama's missive telling me of Alessandra's imminent . . . er . . . the wedding," she finished somewhat lamely as she cast her new brother-in-law a dark glance. If he saw it, he did not acknowledge it.

"And since I have everyone's attention," Lady Amelia started to say, only then comprehending that Oliver was still at the table. "Er . . , um . . . Oliver, my dear. Would you care to see if the Prathams' lad would care to sleep over?"

"Sure!" Oliver cried at once, starting to leap up from the table. At his mother's disapproving glance, he reluctantly resumed his seat, belatedly adding, "Yes, please, ma'am."

"Then you may be excused to go and request his presence."

"Thank you!" He jumped up from the table, fully suspecting he was missing something, but it was bound to be less entertaining than camping in the attics—as he was bound to convince his mother ought to be allowed—with Jeremy Pratham.

When he had fled the room, Lady Amelia began again. "We have begun to receive wedding gifts for Alessandra and Jeffrey, which of course we must do something about. I don't want anyone leaving this table tonight until we have decided what that is to be." She sat down again, fixing them all in their seats with a firm eye.

"Amelia!" Lord Malcolm scolded. "Can't you women just decide that?"

"I don't think so," she said sternly, turning to Jeffrey, who sat on her right at table.

"I should think it would be obvious," he said, not sure if he was indifferent to, or annoyed by the topic, or possibly his mother-in-law. He was already growing tired of the strained relations that took place at meals, and this was only his second with the family. He much preferred talking horses or fisticuffs with his male relations, or even eating quietly alone, without all this conversation about bonnets and routs, and now gifts. "We'll keep them wrapped as they arrive, with their cards attached, and have them sent back once the annulment is in place."

"I think it would be better to unwrap them. At least then it doesn't look as if you had planned the annulment from the very start," Lady Amelia said.

"Yes, fine," Jeffrey said somewhat wearily. "Now if you will please excuse me, I believe I would care to beg a retirement to the library for some port."

"I'll come with you," Lord Malcolm volunteered at once.

The three ladies left at the table remained sitting, each retreating into their own private thoughts. Finally, Lady Amelia broke the heavy silence. "I have asked Miss Parker if she will stay on to help me with the hot houses. She is most delighted to do so, and after this . . ." she mouthed the word distastefully ". . . *annulment* takes place, she can resume her duties as chaperone, though under certain more strict guidelines, I assure you," she added, giving Alessandra a steady look that promised no quarter. She grimaced for a moment, then said, "My

101

girls, I am so concerned that this will not look good for Alessandra. We must make some sort of pretense."

"What are you thinking, Mama?" Emmeline inquired, leaning forward to plant her elbows on the table.

Her mother frowned at the breach of manners, but just then some servants came into the room and began to clear away the evening's repast. She allowed them time to gather a number of platters and plates, and to light some lamps against the gathering gloom of the night. After a minute she indicated that they should bear away what they had, to give the ladies a few moments to speak privately. When they were gone, she said, "I am thinking that we should have a dinner party. Nothing much, but just a little showing off of the newlyweds. It would be expected. I see no reason why we should not."

"I don't know if Jeffrey would approve," Alessandra said at once, the very idea of a party causing her to shudder. She was feeling too fragile, too uncertain of herself right now, to enjoy a party.

"I don't care whether he approves or not. He entered into this whole affair with his eyes wide open, I am persuaded, so he will just have to indulge me, for I know what is best." She stood, adding sternly, "I will go and inform him and your father right this moment. I intend to have this party in two week's time, so we will need their cooperation if we are to ever get ready in time."

"Can I not talk you out of this?" Alessandra made the attempt even though she knew her efforts were doomed. Mama had *that* look in her eye, the one that said, "The more you fight, the less you'll get."

"You cannot."

"I thought not."

"You thought correctly. Now, go to bed, my girls. It

will be busy days for us ahead, I am persuaded. Oh dear is it nearly half past eight? What was I thinking of to allow Oliver to bother the Prathams at such an hour?" She was gone again, leaving the room, trailing comments as was often her wont.

Alessandra dragged herself up to the room she shared so diffidently with Jeffrey, and put herself to bed, leaving one lamp burning for when he came up. She noticed that the room had been straightened up, and she assumed that Jeffrey's things had been removed from the floor of his wardrobe. Evidently his valet must have arrived. She would have known about that if she hadn't hidden all day in the libary. What was the valet's name? Would he have to be fooled, too, like the other servants? Of course.

She could not sleep, for she was not quite warm. It struck her as funny that having Jeffrey there, on the other side of those thick pillows, they still shared enough heat to make sleeping comfortable and possible. And, too, her thoughts were like little mice that streaked forward unexpectedly to nibble at her consciousness, leaving her restless and unable to relax into sleep.

It was more than an hour before he came up. He moved quietly through the room, only making a little noise when he removed his belongings from his pockets to place them on top of the chest of drawers, obviously trying to be quiet because he thought she was asleep. He found his nightshirt, and robe and slippers which the valet must have provided, and removed to the dressing room.

She felt the bed dip when he returned and after he blew out the lamp. As he settled in under the covers, she wondered if it was rude to let him go on thinking she

103

was asleep.

"Jeffrey?" she said timidly. There were comments and questions that had come to her as she had lain there unable to sleep. Hadn't she decided these issues should be raised when they were alone at night?

"You're awake," he said, not giving the impression he was disposed toward conversation.

"I just wanted you to know that you are free to think of the house as your home while you are here."

"Oh. Er, yes," he said, "thank you. That is very good of you."

"You might need to ask Papa if you want to take out one of the carriages, but other than that I'm sure he means for you to make free use of the stables also, of course."

"Thank you."

"Jeffrey?"

He turned over, facing her. His tone was a little exasperated as his voice drifted over the pillow. "Yes?"

"Did you go to see about the annulment today?"

"Yes. I was going to talk to you about that tomorrow, since I thought you were asleep."

"Well, I'm not," she encouraged him to go on.

"There isn't much to tell. The fellow is starting the paperwork for us. He thought it might be 'quite some time,' as he put it, though he wouldn't explain what that meant. It can be dashed difficult to pin a man of the cloth down on any one point, have you ever noticed that? Anyway, it has been begun."

"Was he a bishop?"

"The man I spoke with? No, he's the vicar at St. Dennis's. The one that married us, that Father Ainsley fellow. I went to see my friend, but it seems he has been

104

sent on some sort of sabbatical to the Holy Land. He won't be back for three months, so then, of course I went on to this other fellow."

"I see," she murmured vaguely, deciding at once that she would not bother to mention that her father had gone to see Uncle Bartholomew the bishop, since she could not be quite sure in what light Papa had presented the concept of invalidating the marriage.

"Good night," Jeffrey said with a yawn as he settled amongst his pillows.

"Jeffrey?"

He gave a long sigh. "Yes?"

"Did you have . . . other plans? Had you intended to marry someone else specifically?" A picture of a pretty girl with blond curls and green eyes flashed through her mind. Jacqueline Bremcott had certainly grown into a fashionable beauty since they had known one another in childhood.

. He did not answer for a moment, causing Alessandra to catch her lower lip between her teeth to keep from blurting the question out again, from demanding an answer.

"Our fathers once had an understanding . . ." he said at length.

"I see." She paused, then said, "I just wondered."

"I have explaind all this to her. She understands."

"I'm sorry—"

"Oh, for heaven's sake, please don't apologize," he said crossly. "This whole farce was not begun by either of us, so I see no reason to be apologizing to each other all the time over it."

The word *farce* made her half shut her eyes, as one would when in expectation of a blow. After a moment of silence, she made herself ask, "Will you marry her, when

105

you are free—?" She bit back the final words "of me."

He grunted, and it seemed he would not answer, but then he said gruffly, "I suppose I will."

"Well." With that one little falsely cheerful word she told herself to swiftly and resolutely push aside any hint of hurt pride or mangled emotions that might still be lingering in her head. She had no right to be feeling anything but a polite interest in the ending of this whole bizarre episode, she strictly lectured herself, and she managed a little chagrinned laugh. The words that passed her lips, however, had a distinctly bitter taste to them, as she said, "Let me be the first to congratulate you. It is nice to know those wedding gifts will still be of some use in the near future to those who have sent them."

He sat up and peered at her over the pillow, his face tight. He said in a rough voice, "I would not be so vulgar as to marry anyone else immediately."

"No, of course not," she said, regretful of the comment the moment it came out of her mouth. It had actually sounded shrewish—as if she had any right to be offended if he loved another! As if she cared. And yet, there was a part of her that said, *see, he* is *rejecting you, and not just marriage.*

"Do you have anything else to ask me?" Jeffrey asked flatly, settling back down onto his side of the bed.

"No. But . . . but thank you for answering my questions," she said by way of an apology.

His voice lost some of its edge. "Good night then."

"Good night."

She could tell that it was going to be a long, long night, that sleep would be a long time coming. How did one turn off the mind and just go to sleep? How did one push aside the tumbling thoughts that screamed out to be evaluated

106

despite one's firmest resolution to the contrary? How did one ignore the presence of a man in one's bed?

No, she would not think about anything tonight. She was too confused, too bewildered and hurt, though she knew she ought not be. Would counting sheep help? *One, two, three, four.* . . .

. . . Two hundred six, two hundred seven, two hundred eight. . . .

"Alessandra?"

"Yes?"

He sat up and peered at her dim outline over the pillows. When he spoke, it was a cross between irritation and sheepishness. "I have slept with two pillows all my life. I find it very difficult falling to sleep with only the one pillow. Would you mind it terribly if I were to take one of the pillows from the middle?" He added quickly, "And of course the fourth one would remain where it is."

"I . . . no, of course not, if it means you can sleep."

"Thank you."

"You're welcome."

She watched him remove the lower pillow, the one that had lain between their lower bodies.

When he had resettled with a happier sounding sigh, she said, "Sleep well, Jeffrey."

"Sleep well, Alessandra."

She rolled onto her side, her hand gripping the edge of the mattress to keep from sliding toward the middle, and began counting where she had left off: *two hundred nine, two hundred ten, two hundred eleven.* . . .

Jeffrey's nostrils flared as he breathed in the scent that hovered in the air. Alessandra's perfume: she did not always wear it, or at least it was light enough that it was not always noticed. There was a soft fruitiness to it; now it left him feeling vaguely hungry. He dismissed the idle thought that he would go down to the kitchens to find a late snack, and his mind turned instead to the strangeness of sleeping in a bed with a female to whom he had no intention of making love.

He could have laughed wryly at the novelty of it, but his mind took a different tack as he recalled opera dancers and lightskirts that had invited him to their beds happily, and not to sleep. He recalled some of their faces, and a good many of their activities, so that he tossed and turned restlessly for what seemed like a very long time, punching his pillows around unsatisfactorily, before he finally fell into an uneasy sleep.

Alessandra gave up on the notion of counting sheep long before she heard the gentle buzzing that signified Jeffrey was no longer awake.

Chapter 10

"Amelia!" a familiar voice rang out, bringing the summoned lady herself from her sunny seat in the southern sitting room. She had gone no farther than the door to that room, when a lady dressed in chocolate brown bombazine coursed into the hallway, where they spotted each other at once.

"Jane!" Lady Amelia said. She had mostly managed to avoid Jeffrey Huntingsley's mother at the wedding, having seen the frosty looks that lady had cast upon her while entering the church on the morning of the wedding, but she had known even then that her respite was not one to be long-lived. "I've been expecting you."

"Then why didn't you call on me?" Jane asked with her usual straightforwardness. It was odd, that straightforwardness of hers: she was that way with everyone, it seemed, but her own husband. Amelia had wondered any number of times how differently the Chenmarth marriage might have been if only they had developed the ability to talk to one another.

Angie came breathlessly into the hallway, having

obviously been outpaced by the visitor. "Lady Hamilton, you have a . . . Lady Chenmarth is—"

"That's all right, Angie. As you can see, our guest has found me. Will you please bring tea now?" She turned to reply to Lady Jane. "I apologize for not arranging to call. It has been rather busy about here for some time," she said with just a hint of tartness. "But, please, won't you come in?" She indicated the sunny room behind her where she had been doing some stitchery in the bay window's light.

Lady Jane, a woman more given to her horses and dogs, might have had the thought that engaging in decorative stitchery was hardly a good enough excuse for not calling, but she did not deign to say as much as Amelia whisked her project into a drawer and bade her to be seated.

"This is very pleasant," Amelia said as she settled on the edge of her chair. She had been a hostess for twenty-six years now, and had no qualms about telling little social lies.

"Nonsense. Don't think I didn't know that you were avoiding me at the wedding," Lady Jane said not unkindly, but with assurance.

"It was a terribly hectic day."

"Do I not know it! My son comes to me one day and says, 'How'd'do, ma'am, I'm getting married,' and three days later he does! If that's not hectic, I don't know my own shadow."

"In what way may I assist you today?" Amelia asked, wishing Lady Jane would get to the point of what she could see was to be more than a mere social call.

Angie came in with tea and cakes, but as soon as she was gone the conversation resumed.

"I came to speak with Jeffrey actually, and that girl of yours. I've decided that it's silly for one old woman to live alone in that huge monstrosity, Huntingsley Hall. I think the children ought to have it. I'll go to the Dowager House."

Amelia pursed her lips, instantly deciding to satisfy her curiosity before she revealed Jeffrey and Alessandra's "little secret." "And what does Lord Chenmarth have to say to the matter? Would he support the household?"

"He does already, so what difference does it make to him?" Jane declared. "And besides, Jeffrey has a very healthy quarterly sum from his father and grandfather both. He could run that household himself, and another besides, if he wanted to."

Amelia leaned forward to offer her guest the tray of cakes, and was pleased to see they were petit fours, Jane's favorites. If anyone needed sweetening up today, it was Jane, especially in light of the news she was about to hear.

"Tea?" Amelia asked mildly, reaching for a china cup even as she glanced toward the open door and wondered when she would ever again be holding conversations in which she hadn't a care whether the servants overheard or not. She handed Lady Jane the cup of tea, then rose and went to the door, leaning her back against it as she closed it, long enough to take a deep preparatory breath. *Jeffrey ought to be the one doing this,* she thought with a scowl, but the naughty fellow was out and about, and she was not about to make Alessandra face a disapproving mother-in-law alone.

Jeffrey received a sealed note from his mother and an explanation from Amelia that she had told Lady Jane about the annulment plans, all at the same moment.

"Come in to luncheon when you have read what she has to say," Amelia said in the blitheful manner that indicated she knew full well there could be nothing congenial in the note.

His appetite destroyed, as he had begun to suspect might be quite a common occurrence in this household, he proceeded to break the note's seal.

Dearest Jeffrey (he read),

You are to call on me. Immediately.

It was simply signed *M*, presumably for "Mother."

"Lord Huntingsley," Winters said from the doorway. Jeffrey looked up.

"Winters! I have not had the opportunity to thank you for tending to my things in the . . . er . . . wardrobe."

"Thank you, sir. When you have a moment I should like to discuss schedules."

"Schedules?"

"Of when you would care to be dressed, sir. When you rise, et cetera."

"Oh, of course," Jeffrey said. Inwardly he groaned. He had been avoiding Winters's hints that this needed to be taken care of for three days, wondering how he was going to incorporate his valet into the strange situation he shared with Alessandra. Winters had been increasingly civil of a morning, in direct correlation to his patent disapproval of his lord's ringing for him when he was wanted. He had always had free run of his master's chambers before, and clearly thought this sharing of a room to be bordering on the provincial. Well, there was nothing for it, Jeffrey would have to give the truth to the man; he knew he could implicitly trust Winters to hold his tongue if he were so bidden.

"Come to my room after dinner, and we'll discuss it."

"Very good, Lord Huntingsley."

As the valet turned to leave, Mr. Cloch came up behind him, and announced, "Lord Huntingsley, Mr. Huntingsley."

The two servants departed, their respective duties done, and Elias sauntered into the room.

"Why so glum?" he called to his brother, crossing the room to join him, his hands in the pockets of his coat in an attitude that said he was apparently most content with the world.

Jeffrey crumpled the note still in his hand, and replied to his brother crossly, "I am to go see Mother."

"In trouble with her already, only five days after the wedding? Is she mad that you did not marry Jackie? I always rather fancied that was Father's plan more than hers."

"She does not say why, but I am to go 'immediately.' I don't suppose you'd care to go with me?"

Elias shuddered, pulling a hand from his pocket to make a gesture of emphatic refusal. "I'd sooner join the army!"

"There's a thought."

"What's the matter, old boy? One would think you'd be transported by joy; wallowing in domestic bliss; dancing amongst the stars—"

"You forget I did not choose to be married. 'Twas thrust upon me."

"Ah well. It comes to us all, you know, like birth, like death. No avoiding it, I'm afraid."

"Spoken like a man who has no intention of doing so himself."

"None whatsoever."

113

They grinned at one another momentarily. It was on the tip of Jeffrey's tongue to explain why his mother wanted to see him, but the thought of going through yet one more inquisition stopped him. He could not help but think that Elias would not approve of his plans for dissolving the marriage.

"So, tell me," Elias said, his voice dropping low as he sidled up to his brother with a wink. "Is there any reason why I should give up my designs on permanent bachelorhood?"

"Cad!" Jeffrey huffed, well aware of the nuance that pervaded Elias's question, and feeling immediately guilty that he had not confided the truth that he remained nearly as much a bachelor as his brother.

"My! Aren't we easily upset."

"There are some things a gentleman does not ask another." Jeffrey retreated into propriety.

"But a brother might," Elias replied, wiggling his eyebrows, undaunted.

"Say one more word and I'll make you go with me to Mother's lecture," Jeffrey threatened, once again half laughing despite himself.

Elias clapped a hand over his mouth and raised the other one to wave a farewell as he dashed for the door.

Elias did not, however, leave the house. Instead, he went wandering about, reacquainting himself with the house he had played in on occasion as a child. He only startled a few servants before Patty was brought to see who was wandering the halls. She knew him, and laughed at his light teasing, a comfortable relationship leftover from boyhood, and promised to see that he was not

114

evicted for trespassing as she shooed him on his way.

He found the old nursery, now a quasi-storage room. And next to it he explored the big room upstairs that they had always called the playroom, but which he now realized was little more than a huge finished attic space. He went to the library and delighted in finding the old, and now terribly tame, medical texts that he and Jeffrey had once snickered over. He recalled the atrium, and the little alcove that gave access to the roof—a favorite spot for testing one's derring-do, the roof—and headed down the corridor that led toward it to pay a renewed visit to that once exalted spot. Toward that purpose, he passed an open door, absently peeking in. Ah yes, the Sapphire Room. And here was Alessandra, sitting on the window seat, apparently staring at nothing. There was a book near her hand, but she was making no effort to read it.

"Cousin Lessie!" he hailed her.

He had startled her, but as soon as she recognized him, she smiled brightly. "Elias!"

"That's not what you used to call me," he said, presuming that her greeting meant he was free to enter.

"Ah, yes. 'E-Liar,' as I recall it."

"I hated that."

"I knew that. That's why I only used it when I was very angry at you." She gave him her hands as he approached, and gently pulled him down to sit next to her.

"What were you supposedly reading?" he asked, picking up the book to glance at the title. He whistled, and read aloud, *"My Journey to India,* by Sir Norbert Underhedding."

The seat in the enclave was built for reclining, so she tucked her legs up under her, her skirts billowing around her, and hung her head in a retiring fashion that did not seem like her at all. She smiled slightly and confessed, "I wasn't reading it."

"I could see that you were not, and who is to blame you? No one should ever have to read anything ever written by a Sir Norbert Underhedding."

He had made her laugh, though it was a wan imitation of what he knew to be her usually vibrant manner. Spontaneously, he reached out and laid his hand over hers. "What's wrong?"

She shrugged, and turned her head a little, unable to meet the inquiry in his eyes. Finally she admitted, "It is hard, waiting."

"Waiting for what?" He was puzzled. Perhaps she had no reason to be exactly a shining bride, but this melancholy was something else indeed.

"Here we have another one who has not yet been told," Emmeline said from the doorway.

Alessandra blushed, and Elias said in confusion as he looked up, "Emmeline? . . . what?"

"They are getting an annulment," Emmeline said flatly, but then her voice shifted to a shade of anger as she added, "I am very displeased with your brother."

"Is this true? An annulment?" Elias cried. At their solemn nods, he asked, "But why?"

"Why does everyone have to get so upset over this?" Alessandra said tiredly. "As long as Jeffrey and I agree, I should think that would be an end to the matter." So saying, she stood, gathered up the book, and claimed, "I must get this back to the library. If you will excuse me." She did not wait for their answer, but rushed from the room.

"But on what grounds? There have to be grounds,

don't there?" Elias asked, stunned, into the sudden silence.

"Nonconsummation," Emmeline said, and, in the manner of one who has spoken an obscenity, her color heightened.

"No! Never say it is so! You mean, they haven't . . . the marriage isn't . . . ?"

"Judge for yourself," Emmeline said gravely, pointing toward her sister's retreat.

"Oh, that is too bad of him . . . !" Elias cried, coming to his feet in agitation.

"In all fairness, I do not believe he means to be bad about it at all. I believe he thinks he is acting honorably." She thought she might tell Elias that Papa was making the two newlyweds share a room, but that was more than she cared to explain or even to articulate. Her face was already warm enough.

"But I still don't understand why."

"But you know it was not a marriage either one sought," Emmeline said with a sigh, coming and taking his arm as she began to play devil's advocate even though she felt much the same as Elias. "If you look upon the marriage as having been conceived to scotch any rumors, and only that, then it does make sense. Since they both have comely features, and monies, and come from titled families, there is no reason for them to stay married. They can both afford to wait for love, and I must tell you that 'twas for love that my parents wed. Alessandra is bound to have some romantic notions about 'true love' that could easily persuade her to agree to an annulment. The fact that *we* think they suit is not enough. Really, what do they know of each other? Do they have any common interests? What if they stay married and then find they do not like each other?''

Elias blenched at this, so that Emmeline recalled his own domestic disharmony, and reached out a hand to pat his.

"Perhaps we . . . *I* . . . disapprove of this plan because I am a little concerned that it will not go so well for Alessandra afterward, socially, as Jeffrey seems to think. I have talked to Papa about this, and he says he will take her to Bath, or Brighton, or even out of the country if need be, to give her that first season and a little town polish, away from quite so many speculative eyes. I just hope it doesn't come to that, though it might actually be more comfortable for her that way. I don't know about that, but I do know we should not interfere in their business,'' she finished on a sigh, a little surprised by her own insight.

"I guess I'll just have to let the news sink in a little. I had this picture in my mind of Jeffrey and Alessandra and the lovely little children they would have together. I believe I am disappointed.'' He shook his head in disillusionment and added, "I suppose after a while that he'll marry that stick, Jacqueline Bremcott. But, I suppose she might produce pretty children just as easily as Alessandra would have done.'' His look said that even though that might be true, he could not like it.

"Lady Bremcott?'' Emmeline asked, a confused pucker coming to her face.

"Yes. Our respective fathers had 'understandings.' But, no, I hope that's not his plan, for if Jeffrey loves Jacqueline then I'm a fence post.''

"Well,'' Emmeline's pinched look faded and she

smiled, "you are certainly not that."

"You say that in the tone of voice used by older cousins toward putrid younger cousins."

She laughed then, but could not deny it. "I have been beastly sometimes to you in the past, haven't I?"

"You have."

She lifted her shoulders and spread her hands, palms upward, and said, "I suppose an apology would not wipe the slate clean?"

"It would not. But if you offered to help me, *that* would do the trick."

"Help you? In what way?"

"I think Jeffrey and Alessandra are calling it quits too soon."

"I will not do anything to interfere in Lessie's concerns—" she started to protest.

"And I'm not asking you to. All I want is that you should *observe*. See what happens, see if they have anything in common. I'll just go along to see this churchy fellow, that one that married them. I'll talk to him. There may be ways of slowing these proceedings down. Given time, and opportunity to get to know one another . . . who knows?"

"Perhaps when Lessie is free, she ought to marry *you*, because you, too, are a romantic," Emmeline said, shaking her head in wry amusement.

"Will you do it?"

"I won't spy, but, yes, I will watch over the two of them. They need help, poor darlings."

"Exactly."

"That you, my irrepressible cousin, agree with me, makes me very nervous."

119

Elias grinned widely. "I should have been a knight, or a Robin Hood, for I do so enjoy coming to people's rescue."

"Even those who do not want it?"

"Especially those who do not want it."

"Recall that Robin Hood went to prison for his crimes."

"Recall that he did not stay there."

She laughed again, giving up the fight, for there was not and never had been a hope of winning an argument with Elias.

"Come in, my dear boy. Would you care for tea, or perhaps something stronger?" Lady Jane greeted her son. She had not waited for him to be shown into her parlor, but rather had come out to the hall to gather up his arm and tuck her own through his. She personally escorted him into what he, for a fraction of a second, thought of as the spider's web. At her inquiry, he mumbled something about wanting nothing to drink.

"Mother, you sent me a note," he said, cutting to the issue at once the minute the door was closed behind them.

"Do you know what Lady Hamilton told me this morning?" she asked as she spread her skirts, settled in a Queen Anne chair, and reached to pour herself a glass of ratafia.

"I do. She told me you had called, and what you discussed."

"I was very shocked to have to hear such news from her rather than from you," she said in her deep voice, slightly scolding. "You could have told me what you intended when you called on me before the wedding."

"In truth, ma'am, I did not know my intentions at that time."

"I see," she said, making a tiny moue with her mouth that showed his comment had been unforeseen. She lifted her glass to her lips and sipped daintily, then lowered it to the table carefully and said, "You think I have asked you to come here that I might upbraid you for your decision."

He nodded.

"That is not the case at all. Honestly, sometimes you and Elias make me out to be a harpy, all snippy-snappy and disapproving, but that is not true, I assure you," she said indignantly, though her expression remained sedate. "The truth of the matter is, that I asked you to come to me that I might tell you that I believe I understand, and that I can even approve."

"You do?" he said, now moving to sit down as well. His eyebrows had risen up under a light-colored lock of hair that fell across his forehead, and his response was frankly incredulous.

"I do. If you don't want the girl, get out while you may. Lady Amelia has given me to understand you are supposedly not having relations?" she said it as a question, her dark eyes looking at him intently.

He frowned, and gave a quick nod.

"Good. I advise you to keep it that way if you don't want the marriage. It is the only way you will ever get an annulment. An annulment is one thing, a divorce another. Look at your father and I, and you two boys. All caught in the middle, for years now. The way we go on is bad enough, but a divorce would be worse, at least socially."

121

"I know this."

"So you have opted to end this marriage before any harm can be done. That is good. You are clever."

"I hope so." He stood. "Did you have more to say? I do not mean to be rude, but I have an appointment to see Father's barristers about the estates, and I shall be nearly late as it is."

"No, that is all I wanted to say." Her look softened, and she caught up his hand, holding him for a moment before he could go. "Jeffrey, I want you to be happy. It is a terrible thing to be together, yet separate."

A vision of the bed with the pillows down the middle formed in his mind, but he quickly pushed it aside. He raised her hand to his lips and kissed it, then bent to kiss her cheek.

"I'm glad you understand, Mother. I fancy there could be nothing worse than being married to the wrong person."

"There is one thing," she said, her face paling and her eyes clouding over.

He quirked his head at her, inviting her to elaborate.

His happiness was important, important enough to her that before she could retreat into the old habit of hiding her feelings from her offspring, she answered, "The only thing that is worse is to love the one to whom you are married, and to have them not love you in return."

His mouth came open slightly, their eyes met for a fraction of a second in honest appraisal, and he saw in astonishment something he had not known existed. He blinked and it was gone, for now it was just his mother's usual shuttered brown eyes staring back at him.

He bowed, in a strangely courtly fashion, and released her hand. "Please accept my apology that I could not stay longer." He stepped back a pace, still looking into her now unreadable face. Again his head quirked to one side, and he said, "I feel this is a place where both Alessandra and I could be comfortable visiting while we await the conclusion of these proceedings. May we call upon you?"

"Of course you may," she said. It was hard to know what she was thinking: he thought she was pleased that he cared to call on her again in the near future, but, too, there was something in her calm, half-smile of one who was world-wearied.

"Thank you," he said.

"My pleasure."

"Good day."

"Take care, my boy." She lifted her hand to throw a small kiss at his retreating back, resenting with renewed and embittered energy the long-standing invisible walls that had sprung up between the members of the household she had once shared with her husband.

Chapter 11

"Will there be anything else, my lord?" Winters asked. He stood near the door, his master's cravat and boots in hand.

"No, that will be all."

"Very good, my lord. Good evening."

"Good evening, Winters. Don't forget that new shaving soap I want to try in the morning."

The valet acknowledged this with a short bow, and left, closing the door quietly behind him.

"So you have finally met the redoubtable Winters," Jeffrey said across the cribbage board to Alessandra, his voice droll.

"Redoubtable? I did not realize. I must remember to be in awe of him," she said in an equally whimsical attitude.

"You must. I could never dress without him, and there are others who would steal him away if they could. But none shall have him, for they do not know the secret is that one must pay the redoubtable Winters in the pure coinage—even as I do—of nothing less than Reverence."

"Heavens! I should hate for you to walk about clad as a

clod, so I shall be properly respectful." She laid down her cards, and counted out, "Fifteen, two; fifteen, four; fifteen, six; and a run makes it nine." She reached for the board and moved her peg with glee, very near to winning.

Jeffrey scowled at the cribbage board and then at her cards. "Where is the third fifteen?" he challenged.

She moved three of the cards from her hand next to the starter card.

"Huh," he grunted as he acknowledged the combination.

"I am glad that you explained our situation to him. It shall make it easier to go on."

"Yes, it should," Jeffrey said. He seemed vaguely aloof tonight, leaving the brunt of the conversational effort to Alessandra.

"Anyway, allow me to return to the plans for the supper party. Mama says we are to dine formally, and that will be followed by dancing. I tried to talk her in to an alfresco luncheon, but she would hear nothing of the kind. She says that since we had no prenuptial parties this one must be very proper and staid and overdone."

"I'm sure she knows best," Jeffrey murmured, laying down his hand. "Fifteen, two; fifteen, four; and a pair is six." He moved his peg, then scooped up his crib hand. "Nothing! My crib was robbed," he said in congenial disgust, turning over the cards so that she could see them.

"Worse luck," she sympathized as she picked up the loose cards and the bulk of the deck and shuffled them.

He sat, a blanket wrapped over his evening jacket, his elbow propped against the arm of the chair, his head resting in his hand as he stared into the fire. He watched the flickering flames, not very interested in the game, the bantering chatter more difficult to maintain this evening.

"Jeffrey?"

"Hmm?"

"Your cards." She made a small motion, pointing to his cards lying face down on the table.

He made no move to pick them up. "Something . . . extraordinary happened today," he found himself saying, though he had not intended to speak his thoughts out loud.

Alessandra let the hand holding her cards settle in her lap as she looked toward him, her interest piqued by the seriousness of his tone. "What was that?"

She was looking at him with that same frankness that he was coming to know could disconcert him a little. There was something so genuine about her. She had the kind of demeanor that left one feeling awkward for not being as direct oneself. Somehow he found himself deciding it could do no harm to tell her what had actually been disturbing him all day. "I went to call on Mother today. We spoke of marriages—you'll be surprised to know that she approves of the annulment, for she does not think much of loveless arrangements."

Alessandra nodded, choosing to say nothing. What could she say? This marriage was as unfounded on love as Aunt Jane's apparently had been.

"But, while I was there," he said, his eyes looking inward, remembering the moment, "I saw something. It was there for just one moment, yet I would swear I saw it."

She said nothing, waiting, vaguely pleased that it was not of themselves they were speaking for once, that he was sharing something personal with her.

"I saw, in her eyes, that she loves him. I never knew that she loved him. I have to wonder, how long has it

127

been so?" His hand slipped around his chin, so that now his forefinger rested over his upper lip. He looked into the fire as if it could tell him the answers to questions that kept forming in his mind. He turned his head, looking to Alessandra. "What should I do? Should I tell Father? Would Father care? Should I rather just say nothing, pretend I saw nothing? She said . . . she said that it is a terrible thing to love someone that does not return that love."

Alessandra leaned forward, setting her cards on the table, and reached to touch his hand which lay in his lap atop the blanket. "In truth, I don't know. The only thing I can think to say is that perhaps you should go to your father and see if this sentiment is also in his eyes. Maybe then you could tell him something of what you know. Or maybe you will see that it is wise to remain silent."

They sat still for a moment, he aware of the honest concern on her face, the diminutive size of her hand against his, the precarious talk. Precarious? Yes, that was the proper word. He tried to imagine any other woman he knew in Alessandra's shoes, and failed. She was unique in her ability to stand outside the situation, to let her own concerns be overridden by others' worries. He spoke of love and the lack thereof, and she did not turn away from him, or deride him for his consternation, nor ask him what they were supposed to know of love, these two who meant to separate.

All at once he realized how unreasonable she could have been over this whole sordid annulment business. She could have cried, and raved, or ranted. She could have claimed her honor was being trampled upon. She had not fussed once about her reputation, nor tried to

The Publishers of Zebra Books Make This Special Offer to Zebra Romance Readers...

AFTER YOU HAVE READ THIS BOOK WE'D LIKE TO SEND YOU 4 MORE FOR *FREE* AN $18.00 VALUE

No Obligation!

MORE PASSION AND ADVENTURE AWAIT... YOUR TRIP TO A BIG ADVENTUROUS WORLD BEGINS WHEN YOU ACCEPT YOUR FIRST 4 NOVELS ABSOLUTELY *FREE* (AN $18.00 VALUE)

Accept your Free gift and start to experience more of the passion and adventure you like in a historical romance novel. Each Zebra novel is filled with proud men, spirited women and tempetuous love that you'll remember long after you turn the last page

Zebra Historical Romances are the finest novels of their kind. They are written by authors who really know how to weave tales of romance and adventure in the historical settings you love. You'll feel like you've actually gone back in time with the thrilling stories that each Zebra novel offers.

GET YOUR FREE GIFT WITH THE START OF YOUR HOME SUBSCRIPTION

Our readers tell us that these books sell out very fast in book stores and often they miss the newest titles. So Zebra has made arrangements for you to receive the four newest novels published each month.

You'll be guaranteed that you'll never miss a title, and home delivery is so convenient. And to show you just how easy it is to get Zebra Historical Romances, we'll send you your first 4 books absolutely FREE! Our gift to you just for trying our home subscription service.

BIG SAVINGS AND FREE HOME DELIVERY

Each month, you'll receive the four newest titles as soon as they are published. You'll probably receive them even before the bookstores do. What's more, you may preview these exciting novels free for 10 days. If you like them as much as we think you will, just pay the low preferred subscriber's price of just $3.75 each. *You'll save $3.00 each month off the publisher's price.* AND, your savings are even greater because there are never any shipping, handling or other hidden charges—FREE Home Delivery. Of course you can return any shipment within 10 days for full credit, no questions asked. There is no minimum number of books you must buy.

4 FREE BOOKS

TO GET YOUR 4 FREE BOOKS WORTH $18.00 — MAIL IN THE FREE BOOK CERTIFICATE T O D A Y

Fill in the Free Book Certificate below, and we'll send your FREE BOOKS to you as soon as we receive it.

If the certificate is missing below, write to: Zebra Home Subscription Service, Inc., P.O. Box 5214, 120 Brighton Road, Clifton, New Jersey 07015-5214.

FREE BOOK CERTIFICATE

4 FREE BOOKS

ZEBRA HOME SUBSCRIPTION SERVICE, INC.

YES! Please start my subscription to Zebra Historical Romances and send me my first 4 books absolutely FREE. I understand that each month I may preview four new Zebra Historical Romances free for 10 days. If I'm not satisfied with them, I may return the four books within 10 days and owe nothing. Otherwise, I will pay the low preferred subscriber's price of just $3.75 each; a total of $15.00, *a savings off the publisher's price of $3.00.* I may return any shipment and I may cancel this subscription at any time. There is no obligation to buy any shipment and there are no shipping, handling or other hidden charges. Regardless of what I decide, the four free books are mine to keep.

NAME

ADDRESS   APT

CITY   STATE   ZIP

TELEPHONE
(   )

SIGNATURE   (if under 18, parent or guardian must sign)

Terms, offer and prices subject to change without notice. Subscription subject to acceptance by Zebra Books. Zebra Books reserves the right to reject any order or cancel any subscription.   0791O2

GET
FOUR
FREE
BOOKS
(AN $18.00 VALUE)

ZEBRA HOME SUBSCRIPTION
SERVICE, INC.
P.O. Box 5214
120 BRIGHTON ROAD
CLIFTON, NEW JERSEY 07015-5214

manipulate his behavior in any way, nor berated him about where he was going, what he was doing, how he was spending his money. . . .

"I've never given you any pin money!" he cried suddenly.

"What?" she said, almost laughing at the sudden, peculiar statement.

"And I've never taken you anywhere!"

"Jeffrey—!"

"I've been a beast. I can't believe myself!" His hands came together to seize hers. "Alessandra, we may be trying to end the formality of our marriage, but that is no excuse for me to act as if you do not exist."

"I have not felt that way," she said quietly, her eyes falling to the carpet, for her words were not quite true. He had left the house every morning for the last five days, not returning until the evening meal was to be served, never telling her where or how he spent his days.

"I shall remedy this at once. How much do you think you would need for pin money?"

"Papa would give me whatever I—"

"But *I* am your husband. It should be *my* duty to see that you have some spending money."

"But for what would I need money?"

"Ribbons and gloves, and all those gewgaws that females seem to need so unendingly, of course."

She shook her head from side to side, and half-laughed again, "But, Jeffrey! Why should you frank my gewgaws? You would be making an investment in something that could not concern you for more than a few months."

"I'm not worried about that. I don't care to have you or your parents think me a shabby fellow. I want to treat you respectfully. I want to do what's right, even if it's only for a few months. Come on then, how much?"

"Oh, heavens, I don't know. A pound a week."

"Nonsense! Make it thirty."

"Thirty pounds a week! That's too generous."

"I don't care. I like the sound of it. Thirty. It's a good, solid number. I'll not agree to any less."

"But it makes me feel as though I'm being paid a . . . a . . . rental fee!" she cried, becoming distressed suddenly.

His hands tightened on hers. "Alessandra. I happen to know my father sends my mother five hundred pounds a month. And they are not on best terms, whereas I like to think we are. You must think of it as the normal course for married people. Let me do it for you."

It was on the tip of her tongue to ask if it was normal for married people to sleep as they did, but she did not say it. "All right," she agreed instead, pulling her hands free, determined to come nowhere near to spending that much money. She would give him the unspent balance the day the annulment was finalized.

"Good," he said cheerfully. "And it occurs to me, your mother is putting herself to a bit of trouble to see that we appear to have not prearranged the eventual separation, and I believe that I should assist her in this matter. It's only fair to you. Of course, its only been a few days since the wedding, but even newlyweds do not hide from the world forever. Would you trust me to come up with some appropriate places to be seen?"

"Yes," she said, hiding her once again scrambled feelings behind the relative safety of lowered eyes. Why shouldn't they be seen out and about? It was natural for her to feel this surge of happiness. After all, she had come with her parents to London to enjoy the season, so why shouldn't she tingle with excitement to think of doing just that?

"And I think a little sightseeing might be fitting as well. Have you ever been to St. Paul's?"

"Oh, yes, when I was fifteen Miss Parker took myself and a whole party of girls there. It is quite wonderful."

"I have not. You must be my tour guide."

"I would like that," she said, able to raise her eyes again to his.

"Shall we play some more?"

She blinked, then understood that he was referring back to the cribbage game. For a moment she thought he had meant something about "playing at marriage."

That was not an ill-formed thought, actually, she mused to herself as she took up her cards from the table. To play at marriage: that was how she should think of it. What other girl ever had such an opportunity? She could learn something of how it was to live with a man, how couples went on, learning a role in the manner of children playing at "House." There was much that could be gained from the experience. It was obvious that Jeffrey thought well of her . . . he just didn't want to be married to her. Isn't that how "House" was played? Someone played the role until they grew tired and went home for supper. She should try not to take anything too seriously. Have *fun*, she told herself sternly, enjoy what you may.

"Six," she said, laying down a card.

"Fifteen, for two," Jeffrey countered, laying down a nine, and moving his peg forward two more holes.

He assumed the preoccupied frown that never quite left her face that night was due to her concentration on the play of the cards.

She awoke later that night suddenly. Jeffrey's leg was pressed up against hers, warm and firm and alien. Neither his nightshirt nor her nightgown interfered. It was his bare flesh against hers.

She cautiously moved her leg away, resettling farther up on the bed, her head almost touching the headboard, her legs curled up to her chest. Now only her feet were below the level of the one median pillow.

Jeffrey did not awaken at the change, and after a while Alessandra fell back to sleep.

Chapter 12

"I didn't know you play," Jeffrey said, leaning on his mother's pianoforte.

Alessandra smiled up at him, still playing, her fingers moving in the correct patterns even as she spoke. "I enjoy playing."

"Jeffrey sings well," Lady Jane said from her seat next to Alessandra on the two-person bench. "This deep voice of mine can only croak, but I tell people I am singing the alto part, and most of them believe me. Shall we?"

Alessandra played and they all sang "The Rose That Blooms in Winter" and "Ye Brave Young Men" and several songs well known from Sunday Services.

"You do have a nice voice," Alessandra said to Jeffrey, looking up at him as her fingers idly tinkled across the keys. He looked up from the sheet music he had been thumbing through and smiled at her.

"Thank you," he said.

Her heart skipped a beat, making her stare for a moment. Then she focused her eyes downward, on her fingers against the keys as she began to play again, something—she could not have said what—from Bach.

She had never had a smile affect her in such a way. It had been a simple enough thing, but perhaps it was the . . . the what? . . . the *affection* she had seen in his eyes. He had been genuinely pleased to be complimented by her.

There was something about this suddenly realized ability to please another that made her feel . . . powerful? . . . fortunate? . . . clever? . . . *something*. She had no word for it. But it had been momentarily heady.

Of a sudden, loud screeching sounds, very like screaming, came from the kitchen. Completely composed, Lady Jane rose at once and left the room.

"The chef. His usual afternoon tirade. Pay no attention. I assure you, I do not," Jeffrey explained to Alessandra, moving to take the seat next to her that his mother had just vacated. "You play very well. Shall we play together?" he suggested.

She moved over a little, that their legs would not touch, not even the fabric. "You play also?" she asked even as she mentally scolded herself. What was she doing, behaving so missishly? Even if this man was not in truth a husband to her, he was a cousin. She need not blush and stammer and act a fool just because she found herself unexpectedly alone with him, just because he gave her a smile. She need not let her mind wander over and over the very real fact that they were ever so much more dangerously alone in their room, in their night-clothes, in their bed.

Their loveless bed, she quickly amended, her spine stiffening, her fingers forgetting to play for a moment.

"I play a little. I am very poor at it. Mother made me take lessons, but for some reason the music masters always kept quitting," he answered, grinning at her. This was a laughing smile, a public smile. It did not affect her the way the other had, except to make her put aside her tumbling thoughts and ask laughingly, "Were you very terrible to them, poor fellows?"

"Awful. Here, let us play this," he said. He reached to place the sheets before them. "I, the harmony; you, the melody. One. Two. Three. Four," he counted them down, and they began to play the simple piece together.

At the end, they were not quite together, but he said, "That's not bad, considering we've never tried to play together before. Shall we . . . ?" he indicated the music still before them.

Lady Jane returned, choosing a chair by the fire as she listened to the music and watched them play. Jeffrey was being nonsensical, putting in extra flourishes that did nothing for the piece but which made them all laugh.

When they finished, Lady Jane cried, "Do it right, Jeffrey! And none of those namby-pamby music lessons tunes, either. I want to hear Mozart."

Jeffrey groaned. He and Alessandra sifted through more music sheets, discarding many choices, until he finally agreed to a not-too-complicated staccato passage.

"Hmph! Too military!" his mother sniffed when they had finished.

"Yes, but it required only a minimum amount of skill on my part, which—you must agree with me on this— 'twas as well."

"I thought you played well enough," Alessandra said.

"Oh, Mother! See how she wounds me!" Jeffrey cried, clutching a hand to his heart. " 'Well enough,' she says. I might as well break all my fingers, for I shall never play again." So saying, he laid his head on his fingers atop the

135

keys, striking a strident chord.

"Some wounds are well deserved," Lady Jane said dryly, but she was smiling and shaking her head at his foolish playfulness.

Jeffrey sat up and moved from the bench to survey the tea cart his mother had had sent in when her guests arrived. "Cook all right?" he asked as he selected an orange segment and popped it in his mouth.

"Oh, he's fine. It seems someone moved the scallions from their normal place in the pantry."

"Bad business, that. I'm surprised he didn't quit."

Lady Jane came as near to a snort as a lady could.

Jeffrey turned to Alessandra. "Do you care for anything further?" He made a sweeping motion over the tea cart.

"No, thank you."

"Then let us return to New Garden Hall. I am sure your mama is in a tizzy because it has been," he pulled his watch from his pocket and consulted it, "three hours since she conferred with you about this dinner party of hers. If we stay one minute longer, I suspect she will have the Bow runners looking for us."

Alessandra rose and crossed to her hostess and temporary mother-in-law. "Mama seems to feel that I need to be consulted on every detail," she explained, bending to place a farewell kiss on Aunt Jane's cheek.

"Since 'tis in your honor, well she might," Jane said, kissing the girl on the cheek in return. To her own surprise, she discovered that the little show of affection that she extended the girl was not dictated by any conventions, but by its own sincerity.

They made their farewells, riding away in one of Lord Malcolm's gigs, as the day was pleasant. Lady Jane stood in the frame of her open doorway, chewing absently on a fingernail, a brooding almost-frown creasing her forehead until Jimms, her butler, cleared his throat and recalled her to herself.

"Jeffrey, my boy! Good to see you. Come in and see what I've purchased," his father greeted him heartily, showing him the direction of "in" by throwing an arm to point toward his conservatory, completely ignoring Jeffrey's comment of, "I really just came by to chat a bit."

Lord Richard followed his son down the hall, and announced happily as they passed through the door, "You see!"

"A billiard table! One of your very own? What was the matter with the two at your club?" Jeffrey asked, shaking his head in amused disbelief.

"Why, the very fact they are at my club, of course!" Lord Richard walked over to his table, giving the mahogany wood a loving stroke. "Just think, this way, whenever I can't sleep, I can come down here and sharpen my skill. I'll soon be as good as any trickster, just you wait and see."

"A desirable skill, I'm sure," Jeffrey said dryly.

"Care to play?"

"Well, I was hoping to talk. . . ."

"You cannot talk and play?"

"Of course," Jeffrey assented, just a little exasperated. He removed his jacket, and selected several cue sticks, assessing their lines carefully. How did one go about finding out if one's father cared at all for one's mother? He delayed figuring that out by saying, "Do you think this one is bowed?'' He handed a stick to his father.

''Never say 'tis! 'Tis brand new.'' Lord Richard scowled down the stick, growling in a fashion that was not too difficult to interpret and would have sent the manufacturer into throws of despair.

He selected a different cue stick for himself, setting the one in a corner for later testing and evaluation, and they began to play.

''I took Alessandra to see Mother this morning,'' Jeffrey said by way of opening the conversation.

''Did you? She was a sweet little thing, as I recall. A beauty now. I always rather fancied Alexandria,'' Richard said, grimacing when his shot failed to make the carom.

''Ale*ssandra*,'' Jeffrey corrected, swallowing down the ''And do you like Mother?'' question which sprang unbidden to his lips. However, to keep the conversation going in that direction, he said instead, ''Mother maligned my abilities on the pianoforte.''

''Can't fault her for that. You play the pianoforte worse than you play billiards,'' Lord Richard said, and barked out a laugh.

Jeffrey smiled a little. ''She asked how you were,'' he lied, and cocked a triumphant eyebrow at his father as he took his shot and his cue ball successfully completed the carom for the first point.

''Did she?'' Lord Richard paused to chalk his stick, some of his bonhomie attitude slipping away as he gave his son a level look.

''I told her you were fine.''

''As I am.''

''Now I'll be able to tell her that you play billiards at night, in secret.''

138

"Now why would you want to do that?" Lord Richard leaned on his stick, gazing evenly at Jeffrey.

"I don't know. Why would I want to do that?" Jeffrey said, just as evenly.

Lord Richard sighed and laid his cue stick along the edge of the table. "What are you trying to do here?" he said, leaning his hands against the table's edge.

"I'm not trying to do anything. But I will tell you what I've been wondering about."

"Which is . . . ?"

"Alessandra and I married only to save her reputation. Now we are getting an annulment. No, before you say anything, let me assure you I have already been talked to, and scolded over, and even been given some approval for this decision. There is nothing you can tell me that I have not already been told.

"My point is this: If we had to, she and I could live together for the rest of our lives, with a few simple rules and a little common courtesy to guide us. And we would be largely happy, I believe.

"So. I find myself wondering how it is that my parents cannot strive to maintain this same semblance of peace between them."

He saw the instant anger in his father's eyes, and felt the indignation that he could only expect coming across the table to make his own eyes narrow.

"You, boy? Married six days, and you wonder how such a thing can be? You, who plans to leave this little wife of yours behind practically at the altar, dares to question me?" Lord Richard said in a cold voice. "Why should I answer any question of yours?"

Jeffrey drew himself to his full height, on a par with his father, the conversation having turned all wrong, yet still he felt that at long last he had to know, to understand. "All I want to know is: why did you ever marry her in the first place? Did you not know that you did not like her? You knew each other a long time before the wedding."

They stared at each other fiercely, the one very like the other in appearance and in their nearly identical expressions of anger and hurt.

Lord Richard was the first to lower his eyes, shaking his head slightly, sadly. "I am going to tell you something you may not care to know."

"Tell me."

The older man took a deep breath, then said, "We had to get married. Your mother was already expecting you."

Jeffrey felt the blood leave his face, only to flood back a moment later as he said disbelievingly, "I suppose I should be grateful that you decided to make me legitimate."

For a moment he thought his father was going to strike him, but the clenched fist relaxed after a moment, and the purple vein in his forehead ceased to stand out. "Yes, you should be. It has made your life a lot easier, believe me. And it would not have been honorable to turn away from your mother at such a time." He paused and sighed, a heavy silence falling between them, one that he sought at once to dispel. "But, Jeffrey, lad, do not misunderstand that just because you were started before the vows were made that I am any less proud of you. You are my legitimate son, my heir. I am gratified to see the kind of man you have become." He sighed again heavily, and said, "And so now you know why I married her. But you still do not know why I do not live with her."

"Why is that?" Jeffrey asked hollowly, trying to comprehend a whole new facet of his own birth that had never occurred to him before.

"You saw how we fought. I think the fighting started the day of our hurried wedding. I should have been more bold, less tentative in how I greeted the marriage. I should have never let a rift begin, much less grow. I should have seen how your mother was . . . unsure. Frightened. She is not one to be rushed."

"I would have to say that is not necessarily true, given the facts of my conception."

"Don't be flippant with me, my boy. I'm man enough to knock you down still, if I choose to."

Jeffrey said nothing, his jaw clenching. He had not come there to learn startling news of his own past, but to understand his parents'. He did not need, or want, a lecture from his father.

"And as to this annulment idea. I can't tell you if I think it's crackbrained, or demmed smart. This marriage to a Hamilton is a good alliance. You two have much to offer each other. Not as good as the one with the Bremcotts would—" He saw something in Jeffrey's face and cut himself off abruptly, giving Jeffrey to understand that the discussion had just taken another drastic turn off the course he had wanted it to take. Lord Richard cried, "Well, demme me for a fool! The Bremcott alliance could still go forward if the other is put aside, couldn't it?"

"I think it could," Jeffrey said with an uncomfortable-looking set to his mouth, rather as though he had just taken a bite of something that he suspected had turned foul.

"Well then, that's an end to the matter, I see. We'll be telling the world that 'true love' got in the way of the other marriage, once it's annulled. Oh, it might cause a sensation for a little while—might have to send you off to do the Tour before you marry the girl—"

"I've already done the Tour," Jeffrey said dismissively, "but what I really want to know is how—"

"Only half so, because of that despot, Napoleon. But that's not the point: the point is we'll have the Bremcott estates tied right into our family after all!" Richard cried jubilantly.

Jeffrey did something that he had never done before when he ground out between suddenly gritted teeth, "I don't give a tinker's demme about the Bremcott estates!"

His father stared, startled, his face flushed an uneven red, even as Jeffrey stared heatedly back.

"D'you mean to tell me it really would be a love match then?" Lord Richard asked, obviously disbelieving. "That's why you want the Bremcott gel?"

"Yes! No! I don't know," Jeffrey cried. He threw his cue stick down on the table and strode across the room to seize up his jacket and his tall beaver from the bookcase near the door. He bowed curtly to his father, and said stiffly, "No wonder Mother can't live with you. You are impossible to talk to. I will call again when I have news. Good day to you, sir."

Lord Richard watched him go, utterly perplexed. "Now what the devil was that all about?" he said aloud to himself, scratching at his ear, a look of complete puzzlement on his face.

Chapter 13

"Please pass der butter," the Baron von Brauer said to Alessandra.

She reached for the little silver tray, and as she lifted it the silver butter knife, liberally smeared with the substance for which it had been designed, slid off and fell squarely in her lap. With a small cry she delivered the tray to the baron, picked up the knife, wiped it on her napkin, and handed it on to him with a tremulous little smile of apology. She then attempted to brush the instant greasy stain away with her napkin, only, of course, succeeding in making a larger stain exactly in the middle of her skirt.

"My lady, is dere any vay I can help?" the baron asked, aware of her upset.

"Thank you, no," she said, managing to maintain the listless little smile. It had been a very long meal, one that was almost over. She looked down the table to her husband and her mother-in-law, wondering if she could catch the eye of either, and not knowing exactly what she would do if she did. That end of the table (in fact every part of the table but her own) seemed engaged in stimulating and congenial conversation.

"I did just der same ting, in Vienna one time," the baron said in his friendly, rounded accent, keeping his voice low for her ears alone. "I vas tempted to vear a napkin all evening, but of couse I could not." He laughed softly.

"What did you do?" Alessandra asked.

"I vent to my rooms, changed, and came back, of course. But since I knew der change vould be noted, I made sure it vas a *complete* change, from formal black to bright blue vit der striped vaistcoat and stockings, making a great deal of der butter incident. My choice vas very daring for der evening, I must say, but der Princess thought it vas charming, and I believe I almost started a trend dat evening."

Alessandra's second smile was more sincere, to let him know she appreciated his kindness. The vicar's son on her right had scarcely had a word to say to her all evening, his eyes and his attention on his supper. But that was to be excused, for he was young, young enough that it had crossed Alessandra's mind to ask if he would care to join Oliver at his meal upstairs in the nursery.

She looked glumly down the table again, aware of her spoiled gown and her neglected dinner, and aware that Jeffrey was engaged in some kind of lively conversation between his mother and Jacqueline Bremcott, his dinner companions. Jacqueline was regaling them with some tale that had Lady Jane asking questions even as she laughed, and Jeffrey was smiling, leaning forward as though not to miss a word.

"Excuse me," she said to the baron as she started to rise, "I am going to steal from your idea."

144

"Panache, my dear. It is der secret to life in London," he said with an indulgent smile. She was a nice young thing, pretty, too. She seemed sad tonight, though, and looking down the table at the way her newlywed husband's company was monopolized, it was no wonder. Fie on these customs of sitting host and hostess at opposite ends of a room! In Germany he did as he pleased, for he was master of the lands around his estate, but then there was not this social competition that made up the main thrust of London society there either. There were none to gainsay him in his *schloss*, but that was not so here.

"I must beg your pardon," Alessandra was saying aloud, as several heads at the table turned to see why she had risen. "I have quite spoiled my gown. I must change, and will join you all in the ballroom upon my return."

There were several murmurs of "of course, of course," one or two puzzled looks that said such behavior was on the edge of what was acceptable, and her mother's gay little call of, "What a marvelous time for the ladies to refresh themselves!" So saying she rose also, and added, "Ladies, please feel free to either follow Alessandra and myself upstairs, or Lord Hamilton and the gentlemen to the ballroom. The gentlemen will kindly inform the musicians that the dancing will begin soon."

"No port?" someone muttered, overheard by Alessandra as she moved toward the stairs. Her mother was right behind her.

"Oh, Mama. I hope I didn't upset your evening's plans," she said when she was sure they were out of earshot. Several ladies were trailing up the stairs after them, but far enough behind to allow them a few quick words in privacy.

"Quite all right. I rather prefer the gentlemen to be put

to dancing at once anyway, before they have a chance to drink any more and become even more drowsy on us. And only look at that stain! I hope it will come out. But of course you must change, you could scarcely walk about so! I daresay there was no way other than the way you chose, taking the bull by the horns and announcing your very intentions. Very bright of you, my dear," she commended in a low voice.

"Actually, it was that kind Baron von Brauer's idea."

"He is such a gentleman, isn't he? Of course he's quite a bit older than you, but perhaps we should see about a connection there, after the you-know-what."

Alessandra was shaken, her foot stumbling over the last step up the stairs as she gazed up at her mother. There was no reason to feel so stricken by the very thought that Mama could be considering the baron for her. It had been clear from the moment of her birth that she was to marry *someone*, and since Jeffrey was putting her aside, it was only right that her mama should want to protect her interests by seeing another wedding come along posthaste. It was perfectly proper, perfectly understandable. Nonetheless she could feel the lack of color in her own face as she said weakly, "I . . . I am sure I shall want some time to . . . to not be married."

"Oh, of course," Lady Amelia murmured quickly, just as several ladies stepped up to the landing to join them. "This way, my dears. Would anyone care to have lemonade sent up, or tea, perhaps?"

The other ladies turned left, but Alessandra hung back turning to the right, moving in a heart-heavy manner to the Sapphire Room. There she washed her face in water from the ewer and basin near the bed, and patted herself dry with fresh linen. She sat down on the bed with a sigh, her head hanging slightly, when she heard a sound. She looked up quickly, and saw that Winters had just come from the dressing room.

"My lady," he said, his face flushed and in a little less than its normally correct and void-of-opinion setting.

Another person came from the dressing room: Patty. She had a flushed look as well. "Mr. Winters and I were working out the dressing schedule, my lady," she said at once to Alessandra.

Alessandra blinked, not fooled for a moment. It was not the first time she had seen servants engaged in a little flirtation, but it seemed especially infused with quirky humor in this particularly loveless room. A caustic laugh bubbled behind her lips, but she managed to say merely, "Indeed?"

"It seems the master wishes to be the first to rise, and Roger . . . er . . . Mr. Winters 'ere claims that 'e cannot work wif a lot of people in the room, so I thought as I'd come fer yer every morning at ten? Is that all right, m'lady?"

"That would be fine," Alessandra said, instantly distracted from the budding romance before her. She would have to talk to Jeffrey about this scheduling business. Though it was true she had been quite a slugabed lately, she could not wish to go on that way. She was a country girl, used to country hours. Perhaps she could arrange to be the first to rise. No, that would not work, for how would she bathe? In fact, how did Jeffrey bathe? Surely not in the little dressing chamber, alongside the necessary?

Patty made a hasty and discreet exit from the room, her cheeks still pink as her hand came up to correct the lopsided lay of her cap on her hair.

"May I be of some assistance, my lady?" Winters cleared his throat to ask, his posture and features once again all that he would have them be.

"Where does Lord Huntingsley bathe?" she asked aloud. She was glad Winters knew everything now. It was the only way to avoid having themselves placed, however innocently on Winters's part, in any number of difficult situations. It had proved so far a simple thing to have Angie, who served as Alessandra's maid only when needed, wait for a summons, and to dismiss her when her job was done. But Winters actually took care of his master's clothes and boots and belongings, not to mention his person, and must of needs spend a great deal more time in the Sapphire Room than Angie or Patty ever did.

"Bathe, my lady?" Winters echoed her now.

It had been two weeks since the wedding, and Alessandra could have sworn that at times she smelled fresh soap on Jeffrey as they lay in bed. She had avoided Jeffrey's man out of sheer lack of knowledge of how to go on with him, but that grace period had been erased by the knowledge he now possessed. Trying not to sound as wearied by the day's events as she felt, she elaborated, "I am wondering if I am inconveniencing Lord Huntingsley, so I have asked you where he bathes?"

"At Gentleman Jim's, my lady. He goes a few rounds in the afternoon, and makes use of their facilities there," Winters said, his voice and expression even.

"That's silly," she sighed heavily. She could not like anything that made her even more of a burden to Jeffrey. "I'll talk to him. We'll work something out so that he is not so inconvenienced."

"As you will, my lady."

He bowed and left the suite, and Alessandra moved to the wardrobe to choose another gown. She had been wearing a pale yellow muslin scattered with tiny white bows, really a come-out dress, not one for a married woman. In fact, all her dresses were intended for her first season, nearly half of them white, the rest in pastels. Except the rose silk. She had fallen in love with the patterned fabric the moment the milliner had held it up, and had subsequently been delighted by the way it favored her coloring. She had defied her mama's disapproving glance, and had insisted it be made up. It did not have an especially low neckline, not like the lovely golden brocade that Lady Bremcott wore tonight, the one that had made her own pastel yellow seem insipid in comparison. It did not have the multiple flounces along the hem, nor the sprays of lemon lace that fell from three-quarter sleeves, but it did have a charming underskirt of palest pink, and tiny puffed sleeves that drew the eye to Alessandra's well-formed shoulders, collarbone, and bust. The dress had been made to fit closely from just below the breasts and up, but below there it was allowed to fall in easy, sweeping lines, lines that Alessandra knew flowed gracefully with her when she moved. It only took a moment's contemplation before she pulled it from the wardrobe.

She untied the white bow at her waist, and undid the five pearl buttons at her back, and shrugged out of the yellow cambric. She set it over a chair, instead of back in the wardrobe or in the basket that Patty kept under the bed for used articles of clothing, so that she would remember in the morning to mention the stain to a servant. Her rounded breasts brimmed over her corset, which had been pulled rather tight tonight for the very purpose of setting these particular charms to advantage in her now-ruined evening gown. Her dark hair had been piled high, plaited into an intricate knot by Emmeline, as Angie had not quite the knack for braiding that Emmy had. She knew, aside from her insipid gown, that she looked well enough, though a glance in the mirror confirmed what she had noted, that her petticoats were clinging to her.

She crossed to the stand, and wetted her hands in the basin. She then began to pat the fabric of her petticoats, trying to be careful to not disturb her hairstyle too much as she bent to the task of negating the static.

The door opened and Jeffrey walked in. He came to an abrupt halt, his eyes widening slightly.

"I'm terribly sorry," he said as he retreated behind the door, back into the hallway. "I must think to knock first. Please accept my apologies," his voice came from the open crack just before he closed the door.

She heard his steps as he went on down the hallway toward the stairs, and, belatedly, her heart began to beat erratically. Here was another thing they must work out. Some sort of knock, or a schedule, that they might not walk in on each other in these more private moments.

Oh, it was too absurd! she thought crossly, tromping to the bed to gather up the rose silk, angrily stepping into the gown and pulling the garment up around her waist. *Let the servants know we have separate rooms! Let them talk! Let me have some peace of mind!* she thought in frustration . . . even as she knew she could do nothing to change the way things were, because she had no real say-so, not with Papa. And not with Jeffrey, for he had given his hand on a bargain.

Jeffrey stopped at the top of the stairs, taking a

moment to regain his composure. The event had startled him a trifle, even though in truth he had not seen much of anything, so swift had been his retreat. Only a bit of muslin, a bare shoulder, the curve of a breast, her dark hair piled above a creamy neck. Hadn't he seen much the same kind of scene any number of times in his wild youthful days? It was a moment's thought to recall an illicit occasion or two he had enjoyed, ones where he had stayed to appreciate the view, and where he had not come away feeling distinctly rattled for a moment.

He shook himself mentally, rebuking himself. Only married two weeks, and yet he was increasingly thinking of carnal activity, his mind recalling members of the demimonde he had once known, and married ladies who had cared for dalliance, escapades he had once enjoyed. He experienced, for the fourth time in as many days, the sudden urge to seek out some of the more seedy parts of London, to partake of entertainments there that could be negotiated for by flattering words, or purchased outright. Why shouldn't he? If Lord Malcolm thought him temptable, he would allow himself to be tempted, though not with his pretty little bride. No, he would outmaneuver Lord Malcolm there, and he would not violate the cousinly contract to which he and Alessandra had agreed. But it would harm no one if he visited those who understood those things that required no words, no agreements. There certainly was no reason why he should not.

Yet even as he decided, once again, that there was merit to this scheme, he reminded himself he was married, and that—their understanding aside—such actions would not be very honorable. He was torn, never having agreed to be monklike, and yet resenting his own yearnings. He felt a fool for wanting relief, and he felt a fool for not seeking it out.

His jaw was tight, but his expression composed, as he returned to the ballroom.

When Alessandra had finished dressing, she turned to look at herself in the mirror. She saw a pair of glittering eyes looking out at her. Her color was high, and her dress was flattering. What if the rose silk did not have all the latest fripperies all about it? It was becoming, and she knew it.

She crossed to her jewel case and took out a long string of pearls, which she roped around her neck three times. They had come from Papa on her sixteenth birthday, and they suited the gown perfectly. Next went on the matching earrings, gifts from Mama that same year. As she lifted her hands to fasten the earrings, her wedding ring flashed in her eyes. For a moment she thought about the fact that this ring should have gone to another, and she knew exactly who that other was.

Well, she can have it, and all that goes with it later, but tonight it is mine, Alessandra thought militantly, fiercely. Her eyes darted around the room, taking in the disarray of Jeffrey's comb and brush from where they had been left after he dressed for the evening, saw the bootjack bolted to the floor next to the stool where he sat to have Winters pull those boots for him rather than sully them on the bootjack. She saw the coins, the handwritten notes, the watch and fob that normally made up the contents of the pocket of his jacket. She knew the scent of his shaving soap, of bootblack, and the leather of his driving gloves. She could recreate in her mind the sounds he made in slumber, the way he sneezed, the music of his laughter. These things made up the days and nights of her life for what seemed like forever, not mere weeks. Why should she feel guilty for pretending before their guests that the sights and sounds of this marriage chamber belonged to her? Or was it mere pretense? Hadn't they both taken vows? Yes, the vows were to be put aside, but now, at this moment, everyone believed that Jeffrey and she were together, that they were husband and wife in fact, not just in word.

She had endured the horrendously lengthy meal that had cut her off from most of the gaiety about the table. She had been placed under the scrutiny of the Baron von Brauer's wise eyes, eyes that had clearly noted her unhappiness. She had needed to abide her mama's speculation as to the matrimonial prospects of that same kind fellow, and now lastly had been subjected to that awkward and unplanned entrance into the bedchamber by Jeffrey. These subsequent events had fanned an already smoldering ember of resentment, had heaped coal atop coal fueling the fire that was her sense of ill-usage, until now she was filled with the intensity of angry rebellion and rigid determination. She would return to that ballroom, and she would *not* be ignored. *She* was the bride, the one that ought to be holding court at table, the one whose opinion should be solicited, the one who ought to be flattered and made much of. *She* was Jeffrey's wife, however temporarily, and she would claim whatever rights ought to be hers.

In that righteous and wrathful frame of mind she went down to the ballroom. Champagne, floating in a frothy bath of shaved ice, had been brought into the room and set up on a table pushed to one side to allow for dancing. One of the servants went by with a tray filled with glasses of the drink, and Alessandra seized one as he passed. She looked over the rim as she sipped, learning where people

153

were and what they were doing, her eyes fairly snapping with resolve. The musicians had not yet begun to play, and their strident efforts at tuning suited her mood perfectly. She saw that her papa was talking to the maestro, and her mother was flitting around making sure everybody who wanted one was finding a partner. Jeffrey was in a group of couples, easy to spot because of his height, and standing next to him, her hand lightly on his sleeve, was Jacqueline. So, they meant to open the dancing together, Alessandra thought, finishing her champagne with an indignant, angry gulp. She'd be demmed if they would!

Just as she thought this, Jeffrey turned to Jacqueline, and murmured something. The woman took her hand away, nodding and smiling, and Jeffrey looked up and around. As soon as he spotted Alessandra, he started toward her.

Maybe it was the champagne, or maybe the sudden realization that he was not going to snub her with that woman, but in the space of a heartbeat she felt much less contentious. She felt the set of her shoulders relax, the bubbly champagne seemingly going to her head, making her smile brighten, making her almost croon as she greeted him, "Jeffrey!"

"Are you ready for our first dance?" he asked, as he took her in his arms.

A shiver, totally unexpected, ran down her spine, surely the result of his warm breath on her ear, or perhaps the byblow of her heightened emotions.

They were alone on the dance floor. Another shiver went through her as she realized that she was positively reveling in the fact that all eyes were on them. She felt the wave of approval that swept through the room, knew

154

that they looked well together. Surely they were the very center of the universe, with all the stars and planets smiling down upon them, and she could have stayed so standing that way forever.

He looked over his shoulder, waiting, and finally nodding to her father and the maestro when they failed to take the cue and begin playing. The nod, however, was sufficient, and the strains of a waltz began.

She felt his hand on her back, light, and she felt his hand holding her own. She noticed how he held his arm at the right angle, how he moved smoothly, as a man who had practiced much and well.

"Did you see my father and mother are here, at the same event? Did you see that Father was actually speaking to my mother?" he said, close to her ear again. It was hard to miss the uncertain happiness in his tone.

"Oh, Jeffrey, that is wonderful," she said, her voice dreamy as she silently bid him go on speaking, go on letting her bask in the deep timbre of his voice, the warmth of his touch, the sway of the dance.

"I do not get my hopes up, but, yes, it is something. A start toward reconciliation, perhaps."

Dancing with him was simple, it required no thought. He led and she followed. The telltale pressure of his hands guided her, and even though she had never waltzed in public before, her lessons came to the fore and she felt as though she had been doing it for years. For a minute no one joined them, but gradually couples moved forward to begin to sway about the polished floor, their colorful dress and graceful movements like something from a fairytale. She and Jeffrey said nothing more, giving themselves up to the music, though he did smile at her a few times, smiles that she returned as though she

155

had lost control of her own reactions: moon calf smiles, the result of the intoxication of her presence in his arms.

It was over much too soon. He escorted her to the side, bowed over her hand, kissed it lightly, and murmured, "Thank you for the honor."

Then he was gone, moving to ask another to dance with him for the next set that was assembling, a country dance. It was Jacqueline Bremcott who accepted his hand with a dazzling smile.

Alessandra stood and watched, coming slowly down to earth again, until she felt rather as if she were sinking into the floor itself. It had been an obligation, that was all! That was why Jeffrey had come to claim the first dance with her. It was what was expected. He would do what was expected. Of course, of course. What did she expect? What had she been thinking of?

"Lessie?" Emmeline touched her sleeve. "Are you all right?"

"Oh!" she jerked at the touch and flushed, mortified to think that any of her distress might be showing on her face. "No. I mean yes, I'm fine. It's . . . it's a little warm, don't you think?"

"Perhaps a trifle . . ." Emmeline said uncertainly.

"I . . . I think I shall walk in the garden."

"I'll come with you."

"No! I mean, we can't have you becoming chilled now."

"Peahen," Emmeline chided softly, her face smoothing into a tentative smile. She took her younger sister by the arm. Without further ado, she led Alessandra from the room, out the French doors and into the garden.

The cool night air did feel good, stroking Alessandra's

heated features, hiding her anguish in the gloom. She could not have stayed in that room, not in a million years. She could not have smiled upon the sight of Jeffrey and Jacqueline Bremcott dancing together.

They stood thusly, without speaking, for the space of several minutes. Finally able to slow her whirling thoughts down a little, Alessandra came to think that it was as well that Emmeline had come to the garden with her, for she knew that if she had come out here on her own she would have opted to stay out here all evening, never returning to the dancing, which of course she could not do. She was the bride, the wife, the one being shown. Even though the thought now stung like salt on a wound, of course she would have to go back in to the party.

"I don't know how you do it," Emmeline said into the stillness, her voice concerned, yet familiar and steady and soothing, her hand coming to lay on her little sister's forearm.

"Do what?" Alessandra kept her face averted, staring into the darkness of the garden.

"Bear this foolishness. The party, for one thing. Sharing that room, for another. What was Papa thinking of?"

"He thinks he's doing what's best for me," Alessandra said lamely.

"There's only a shred of merit in the whole absurd idea."

Alessandra said nothing. A sense of tranquility could be restored, she hoped, she prayed, perhaps if she just did not have to speak too much, maintain a false calm too long.

"Ah well, my dear sister. It will be over soon."

Emmeline said this last a trifle sharply, so that at last Alessandra turned to look at her older sister.

"I will remember that," she said, her chin raising a little. Emmeline's message was clear enough: don't forget he does not want to stay married to you.

"I hope so. It would be foolish to fall in lo—"

"Yes, it would," Alessandra cut her off.

Emmeline compressed her lips, realizing there was nothing further to be gained from quizzing the girl. It was clear the exchange had helped Alessandra to recover her poise, that her feet were once again on the ground. "Shall we go in?"

Alessandra nodded, accepting her sister's arm, her face gravely composed.

Inside the ballroom, Jeffrey reached for Jacqueline's hand, their fingers touching lightly as they executed the movement required by the dance.

"You have been to the church?" she asked in a low voice. It was an innocuous enough question, if anyone should have happened to overhear it.

He had not been exactly looking at her, merely assuring himself of the location of her hand as he gazed over her head at the gathering. Now he fixed his eye on her, and after a minute frown had creased his brow, answered, "I have."

It was in his opinion not a discreet question, nor subject. He was a little surprised that she had asked it. Elias had been wrong. Jacqueline was no pattern card; she was not completely predictable, even as she had just proved. Jeffrey could have told him this; he had been in Jackie Bremcott's confidence a long time, since she was a puling babe and he in short pants. He knew much about his longtime neighbor's characteristics, knew she was

158

capable of a number of mischievous or wayward behaviors, but he had not expected her to be gauche.

"I see the Viscount Aldegard was invited tonight," he said, changing the subject abruptly.

"Oh, him," she answered flatly.

Jeffrey looked at her again, in surprise. She usually had any number of nice things to say about the viscount. "Has he fallen out of your favor?" he teased lightly.

"Why, I thought you knew that every man has fallen out of favor with me of late."

His neck grew warm under his cravat. The dance separated them, so that he had a moment to evaluate this strange reaction. It was not as if he did not know that Jacqueline wished to marry him. It had been so for years. But before it had always been subtle; something to think about next year, something he never had quite brought himself to really imagine. The overt way Jacqueline's emerald eyes now pleaded with him to understand what a well-brought-up young lady could never quite say directly, disturbed him.

He knew it was somewhere right around the age of twelve that she had realized she was quite pretty, and had begun to affect a rather frequently imperious manner, including the ability to make men do as she bid just by so little a thing as a glance. He had found himself, on more occasions than he cared to recall, running to do her bidding because of a threatened pout upon that well-shaped mouth. Now he looked down at her breathless, rather expectant expression, and wondered how much of this wide-eyed modesty she displayed was genuine—now that he knew she was capable of discussing annulments and nonconsummations if it suited her purpose.

Perhaps that was unfair of him, he chided himself, for

had she not shown him the way free from a duty that he had not sought and which had been unfairly thrust upon himself and Alessandra? However, he could not care for this feeling she imparted of inevitability, of orchestration.

He resolved at that very moment that he would do whatever pursuing needed to be done. Jackie could play what games she would, but he would not be maneuvered.

He took her to the edge of the dance floor, and looked up in time to see Lord Graham approaching Alessandra. With a quickly murmured excuse to Jacqueline, he hurried to his wife's side.

"Sorry, old chap, my dance," he said, whisking Alessandra away from Lord Graham's arm.

"But we've already danced," Alessandra said, the look on her face strained and far less than receptive.

She thought she understood: here was Lord Graham, who had so effectively caused this marriage by his loud and plentiful reports of the dress-ripping incident at the park. And so here was Jeffrey, showing the very gentleman how well suited the match was after all, trying to put any lasting rumors to rest by his proprietary actions.

She kept herself far from Jeffrey's side, only her hand very lightly touching his sleeve, her thoughts completely incoherent as her sunken heart pounded dully in the pit of her stomach as he pulled her inexorably toward the middle of the dance floor.

"We are married. We can dance together all night, if we choose to be rude," he said, smiling at her. He thought somewhere in the back of his mind, *Alessandra is perfectly safe. She will not make me wonder all night what she is really thinking and saying, will not make me think about implications and indications.* He wanted to dance with her, give himself up to the simple pleasures of moving well and not being chatted up every moment, or of having long-lashed, speaking eyes telling him things he had to decipher to comprehend. Alessandra looked very pretty tonight in this rose gown he had never seen before, and she would allow him to take the leisure of a mere dance, without the penalty of deep, involved, convoluted conversation.

He looked down at her, relief making his smile radiant. It was *that* smile, the one that said so clearly that he was pleased to be with her, at this very moment in time, the smile that took her breath away. Despite her sister's warnings, despite her own resolve, she found herself relaxing, sliding into his arms, casting aside in a moment all her reservations, her expectations of hurtful sorrow and painful perceptions that she dare not analyze. Tomorrow was soon enough to figure out why he could hurt her so; today was for enchantment, however ephemeral. *Could a flower turn from the light of the sun?* she asked in the last distant part of her that was not already lost to hopeless daydreams and mindless exhilaration.

Jacqueline looked on from the sidelines, knowing she had upset Jeffrey. It was clear by the way he flirted so with the wife he meant to put aside. She must remember to not question him; he did not care for that. She had wanted to ask him, "when?" but now she saw this was a subject on which, for now, she must hold her tongue. He wanted this relationship on his terms. That was all right, she understood that, for he had balked with her before. She could let him feel he was leading the way. They had been playing at this contest of wills for years, and she knew the rules well, rules that had always been in

161

her favor.

She looked around the room, searching for a place to be where it was not so obvious that no one had asked to partner her for this dance. There was Peter, the Viscount Aldegard, and there was no mistaking that he was deliberately giving her one minute the cold shoulder, and the next was sneaking glances in her direction.

Her spirits rallied: it would be a simple thing to convince him anew that perhaps he stood a chance with her again, now that Huntingsley was married. Oh, how much more pleasant to have him fawning over her again, instead of this silly business of acting as though he had been mortally wounded by her neglect. She crossed to him at once, and, as she had known would happen, within three minutes he was offering to take her up for a ride on the morrow.

Chapter 14

Four weeks. They had been married four weeks. He had been virtuous for four long weeks. The only part of him that had been active was his imagination, and that seemed to be working to the point of exhaustion. His body was restless, hungry. His mind knew no fewer cravings, and his spirit was tormented. He knew easily enough how to seek out a cure, but he was loathe to do so. Demmit, it wasn't honorable to take a mistress . . . so soon. Yet it was entirely imaginable, so very easy to picture. What was he thinking? Any vows would soon be put asunder anyway; why did he need to feel so fitful? It was surely mere weeks until he was a free man.

It did not help at all that he was surrounded by the trappings of a woman: a corset laid over a chair, a hint of perfume on the pillows he chose for the night, a ribbon that had fallen into his boot. Unforeseen little things that set his imagination dancing, his senses reeling unexpectedly.

Once or twice he had opened her drawers, just to see, just to touch lightly the things that made up her world;

she might have smiled had she known she was not the only one who was experimenting with the impressions of marriage. He had opened her wardrobe, looked at her gowns, her slippers, her half boots, her hats, just to marvel at the daintiness and foreignness of having them in his chambers.

A litany of simple things filled his eyes, his ears, his days and nights. He noted the way she tilted her head when she was thinking, the way she stuck out the tip of her tongue while she was stitching, had seen the little frown that meant she was really listening. He recalled the single dimple that appeared at the right corner of her mouth when she smiled or laughed. He watched her hands, moving so delicately as she talked, and noted the clarity of her speaking voice, with no hint of lisp as was often conceived as fashionable, but which he could not abide.

There had been that day that she had taken her mother's place to go into the countryside and visit their tenants, to see that their appropriate needs were being taken care of. She had spent the whole day at it, bearing castoff clothing and warm foods and kind words where they were needed. He recalled how he had never even thought to mention this to Jacqueline, who had been seated next to him at yet another dinner party, yet somehow the words, sounding rather full of praise, had just fallen out of his mouth. Jacqueline had lifted her eyebrows delicately, in honest puzzlement, then laughed and asked him why Alessandra had bothered herself to do such a thing.

He had blinked several times, thinking it was self-evident, but out loud he had said, "To help her mother and the tenants, of course."

"Well, it's not as though her mother could not go on another, more convenient day. But perhaps she went because she likes to ride?"

"Yes, perhaps so," he had murmured, realizing anew that Jacqueline had been much petted, perhaps even spoiled, in her upbringing. The duties of a landowner's wife toward the tenants had yet to come her way, therefore she could not be faulted in desiring to leave the duty to her mother who would know better how to go about it. . . . At that point his thoughts had trailed away, the excuses making no sense to him at all, so that he refused to examine them any more closely.

Yesterday Jeffrey had found the small reticule in which Alessandra kept her pin money, and a simple glance at the bulk beneath the fabric told him she had not spent much, if any. He had frowned to himself, thinking she either meant to snub him, or that perhaps she did not know what to make of the strange arrangement, did not want to spend his money on things that really could not be considered to be of interest or of investment to him. It flashed through his mind that Alessandra had not taken him at his word, as Jacqueline would have done. He would have to mention again to Alessandra, obliquely, he supposed, thinking of the stubborn light that he had noted once or twice in the set of her eyes, that he truly had no objection to the one who bore his name spending his ready, especially so small an amount as this purse contained.

The day before yesterday he had taken her to the British Museum and to St. Paul's. She had not brought forth her reticule then to buy any of the souvenirs or sketches available. But whereas her money purse may not have flowed freely, she herself had been bursting with commentary, an erstwhile tour guide full of facts and interesting tales. He had teased her lightly about being a bluestocking, only to apologize profusely when she had colored up and held a hand over her mouth. Some more gentle teasing had eventually led her back to another torrent of erudition, during which he had chortled frequently, as they were joined by others of their acquaintance who had doubtless not had so fine a school lesson in most of their collective lives.

Today he had taken her driving in the park, a well-stocked picnic basket at their feet. When she asked he had assured her that it was "not the thing" to be driving as early as two in the afternoon, let alone stopping to spread a picnic blanket, but he could not care tuppence for "the thing" anyway. She had laughed and agreed to be vulgar enough to join him for a picnic there on the hallowed grounds of Green Park. Some persons with raised eyebrows went by in carriages, but others stopped, and some of those joined them in their repast, until they had a merry circle of picnickers gaily consuming the contents of their late afternoon luncheon.

He had looked up, laughing from some jest, from his reclining posture on the grass, had seen her hat tugged away by a sudden, errant wind. He had seen her long hair come loose from its pins to be caught and tumbled in the breeze. He had watched her run after the hat, her skirts pressed tight to her form by the same wind, then caught and lifted to reveal two delicate ankles as she finally captured one of the errant hat's ribbons. She had been breathless, laughing and curtsying as her efforts were applauded, and he had found himself coming to his feet and crossing to her side. He had settled the hat on her head, tying the ribbons for her under her chin. For a moment she had remained still, only her dark hair swimming around her in the breeze, her face raised to his. Then she had stepped away from him, reaching up to move some of the wind-wild hair out of her eyes, laughing again, in a way that was as melodic as her singing.

The only blight on the day had come when they had packed up to go home. It was five in the afternoon by then, and all the fashionables were out and about. He had looked up from where he had been emptying out a glass of wine, directly into the eyes of Jacqueline Bremcott. She was once again placed upon the Viscount Aldegard's phaeton, as she had been seen any number of times lately.

Alessandra looked up and saw the woman a moment later. There was Jacqueline, sitting high on the phaeton, the westering sun backlighting her blond beauty, making it seem almost that she was the source of the day's warmth. Her parasol turned ever so slowly in her gloved hand, her smile was white as pearls; her gown of rich cream lace over pale blue was surely the latest mode, and she was the embodiment of everything fine and feminine, graceful and refined.

Jacqueline and the viscount both offered their greetings, to which Jeffrey jovially responded. Alessandra said nothing, unable to think of a single simple sentence that would not reflect the disenchantment she found in their company.

Jacqueline spoke, her eyes for Jeffrey alone, saying, "What manner of festivity have we just missed, as it appears we have arrived too late?"

Jeffrey explained the picnic to them, his tale receiving cordial laughter, and then they made their good-byes. Alessandra was not the slightest bit sorry to see them go, and felt a moment's satisfaction when Jeffrey had turned, missing the lingering backward glance that Jacqueline had sent his way.

She would not have lost so much pleasure in the day if she had been privy to Jeffrey's thoughts. For although Jacqueline's appearance today had been absolutely striking, her beauty and charm had only led his mind back to an enumeration of all the womanly attributes that living with Alessandra had brought forward into the sphere of his existence. There was no denying her presence in his life, and it was the nights in the bed that were the most difficult to endure. There she was, warm and feminine, usually making small sleeping noises that sent his heart's blood thundering a tattoo against his eardrums. She was as near as she could be, and yet a hundred miles away from his touch. He knew, in one part of him, that these hungers were not his fault, and that he ought not to torment himself because he felt them; there was another part wherein he chided himself for being so base that he could not be comfortably celibate for what was really not such a long time; and there was yet another side that was secretly amused at how well Lord Malcolm had understood the yearnings of a man.

As he handed Alessandra up into their carriage, he thought with a deep sigh that it was time to see that the annulment process was hurried up.

"I'm doing what I can, my lord," the vicar, Father Ainsley, said, looking over his pince-nez disapprovingly.

"I hope that is true," Jeffrey said, returning his look levelly.

"Have you considered what I said when last we met?"

"Have you considered what *I* said?"

"It is just so unseemly. Married one day, and asking for an annulment the next! These things do work out, my lord. There is evidence to the fact all about us. There is no need to be so hasty, to throw away the unknown simply because it is unknown. God works in mysterious ways, as they say."

Jeffrey waved a hand in the air, not wanting to go through this conversation again. "What is unseemly about one day? Would you rather I wait a year? That is, of course, quite ludicrous, my dear fellow. As I said before: better to get this done and over with. You would not care to be the cause of a divorce, now would you? But, come, we've gone over this before. Just tell me how things are going on, and be assured that I have heard your opinion on the matter."

The vicar scowled at the word *divorce,* but said, "You are a determined young man. Very well, but all I can tell you is that I am bringing the facts before the bishop today. After that, I will have more to tell you."

"You're just now going to the bishop?" Jeffrey cried.

"He is a very busy man. One does not snap one's fingers for an appointment of this type, you know."

Jeffrey shook his head in irritation, but he stuck out his hand as he rose to go. "You will send me a note when you know something?"

"I will do that, certainly," Father Ainsley agreed, accepting his hand and shaking it, albeit not heartily.

"Thank you, then. Good day."

"Good day, my lord."

It was not an hour later that the vicar was visited by another Huntingsley. He sat back in his comfortable chair in his poorly lighted office, and spoke to the visitor.

169

"So, you then are Lord Huntingsley's brother?"

"I am," Elias said, nodding.

"And what exactly are you telling me?"

"It's very simple. Jeffrey, my brother, the Chenmarth heir, came to you seeking an annulment, did he not?"

Father Ainsley hesitated for a discreet moment, but then he nodded, his hands intertwined on the desktop, his expression deliberately blank.

"I just wanted you to know that I like him and his wife together, and I think you should slow down this whole annulment process. Give them a chance to get to know one another a little before they go their own ways, there's a good fellow."

Father Ainsley leaned forward with a testy "harumph!" He removed his pince-nez to rub the bridge of his nose, futilely trying to stave off the beginnings of a headache.

His headache was only a trace better by the time he was sitting in the bishop's receiving room.

The inner door opened and a smiling man stepped out, clapping the bishop on the shoulder and pumping his hand in a hearty farewell. Father Ainsley recognized the smiling man at once as the father of the bride at the Huntingsley-Hamilton wedding over which he had presided.

With one last shaking of hands, the father of the bride left. The bishop turned his cherubic face to his underling, indicating his office with a movement of his hand. "Charles!" he greeted his brother in the cloth. "We have a little matter of an annulment to discuss, eh, my good fellow?"

Father Ainsley, rising and moving forward, suspected

the nature of this appointment had already taken a different tone than the one Lord Huntingsley had wanted him to present, and also strongly suspected that his headache was not going to get any better any time soon.

"I'm worried about Jeffrey and Alessandra, sharing that room day after day like they do," Lord Malcolm grumbled to his wife. They were in the conservatory, where Lord Malcolm had incongruously brought all his pistols and rifles for their monthly cleanings.

"Really, Malcolm, I've been worried about that all along!" Lady Amelia cried. "'Tisn't natural. Where do you suppose he's sleeping?"

Lord Malcolm just grunted, pretty sure he knew where, for Jeffrey had not been looking haggard or cold-riddled, so he was bound to be sharing the bed in that cavern which was erroneously called a room.

Many another man would have been sharing more than a bed by now, but there was nothing about his daughter's haunted face that said *that* had happened. In fact, that it had not was what concerned him. What was this doing to Alessandra? Was she innocent enough to walk away from such rejection without harm? He might have thought so once, but now he reamed out the barrels of his guns with unaccustomed and absent-minded energy.

"I didn't tell the bishop that they're sharing a room," he added grimly.

"You can't. You promised Jeffrey you would sign any annulment papers put before you, and there can be no annulment if the church believes they are living as man and wife," Lady Amelia clucked at him, wielding her

171

embroidery needle as fiercely as her husband did the barrel brush. .

Lord Malcolm grunted again, then the brush began to move less methodically. He slowly sat upright, his eyes widening as realization came to him.

"You're right, Amelia. All I ever promised was that I would sign any annulment papers put before me." He leaped to his feet, his eyes shining. "I never said I'd do nothing to prevent those papers from ever being drawn up! The answer is right before our eyes. Amelia, you are a gem!"

"My dear Malcolm," she interrupted him, her needle as sharply poised as the expression on her face. "He'll just deny that they ever . . . you know. Then there will have to be a doctor called in, and that sort of . . . proof may not be what you want. Think of poor Alessandra's humiliation," Amelia interrupted him.

Lord Malcolm slowly sank back down into his chair. "Blast! You're right. But still, it's an ace up my sleeve. I'll use it if I have to. It might come to that anyway."

"Not without telling me and Alessandra first, you won't," his wife said firmly.

"All right. All right." He began to polish his hunting tools again, his eyes half-closed as he considered if—and how best—to use the unsuspected ace he held.

"Right this way, lovey. Mine's the first on the left."

Jeffrey followed the woman down a dim and unclean hallway, into a room that the resident had taken time and trouble to make considerably more pleasant.

She was small in size, and dark haired. Her eyes were brown, instead of more lightly colored as he scarcely allowed himself to know he secretly would have preferred. Her clothes, if such they could be called, were flimsy draperies.

"Yer like anything special?"

He looked about the room. Nice furnishings, but overdone. Too flowery, too feminine. He felt uncomfortable in such a room. "Wine?" he said in a rough voice that did not sound very like his own.

"O'course. Very good, too. I likes a good wine."

She kicked off a shoe, then the other, giving him a hungry look that he did not doubt she had practiced many times. She poured him a cup, and brought it to him, pressing her body along his as an equal offering.

He took the wine, and drank it fast. He threw the cup aside, seeing that her lips were close to his. He bent and kissed her, but it was brief; he could not bring himself to let his lips linger on hers. He might as well have been kissing his own brother, so wrong did it seem. But it was not her lips he wanted.

He had paid his money upfront, as this house required and which people paid because the girls were certified clean by doctors, and he had certainly done this kind of thing before. Of course, that had been in his salad days, which seemed somehow very long ago. But his money was paid, and other appetites seemed alive enough, even though he had no desire to kiss this female. So he had his coupling, short and without any play.

He dressed silently and left the room, not acknowledging her call of, "See yer later, lovey."

As he firmly closed the door behind him, he propped himself up against the dirty wall of the corridor, leaning his head back, his eyes unseeing for a moment. He had not satisfied anything, hardly even his flesh. What a hideous experience. What a demme fool he was. Salad days jollies had seemed so different. No, she would not see him later. No lady of the evening would. He supposed, with a short bitter laugh, that meant he was ready to settle down. Perhaps it was as well that Jacqueline was waiting at the end of all this craziness for him.

He went down the hall and out to his carriage. He arrived at Gentleman Jim's a short while later, and immediately requested a bath, in which he washed for an hour without feeling one whit the cleaner for all the scrubbing he did.

That night in bed, Alessandra told him that she wanted to work out a bathing arrangement. He was oddly silent, brooding almost, but finally he said, "Whatever Patty and Winters work out will be fine."

He rolled over, leaving his pretend wife to wonder in what way she had offended him.

Jeffrey looked down at Alessandra as he pulled on his driving gloves, his coat already in place. He had returned to their room this morning once Angie had come forth, for that was the signal that they had decided meant Alessandra was decent enough to receive him. "I had thought that today we would go to the—"

"Oh, Jeffrey," she interrupted him with an apologetic tone, "Did I not tell you? I have promised myself to Mama and Emmeline for the entire day. We are going shopping, and to the lending library, and to hear a discourse on summer-blooming flowers. Should I tell them I may not go along? It would only—"

"No, no, of course you must go. I'm sure it would be a

lovely day for you," he said at once.

"But I should not care to go if you had plans—"

"Another day," he said brusquely. "I merely thought we might visit London Tower, but any other day will suit as well." He looked down at her uncertain little face, and though a sudden and inexplicably keen sense of having his plans go awry assaulted him, he managed a smile, and said, "Please make free today with the monies I have given you, Alessandra, lest I fear you think me an ogre."

A look of distress crossed her features then, and she flushed uncomfortably. "Th-thank you," she stammered. So he had noted the fullness of her reticule! She had already made up her mind that she was *not* spending his money, not beyond a few middling coins. And she would not do so now, despite his words. She would be just as considerate as he, and if that made him feel like an ogre, well, that was little price for him to pay for the weeks and months she must endure as a half-wife.

He backed away from her, his throat suddenly constricted in the strangest way. He had seen her angered, upset, blinking back tears, amused, disbelieving, and even gay, but he had never before seen her flustered, and this at his own words. Whatever had he said to make her look so discomfited? In what way had he insulted her? Perhaps he had sounded a little curt? He had certainly felt a moment's twinge of pique when she turned down his offer of a day spent with her, but he thought he had not communicated any of that by way of speech or manner . . . but perhaps he had. She was a sensitive creature, for all that she never complained or harped or pouted. He must remember to be the epitome of correctness and politeness whenever they spoke, to avoid upsetting her in these small matters.

It was with such lofty intentions that he mounted his horse, and drove that poor beast across London without a thought for its comfort, nor a more proper pace.

"How nice of you to call on us," Lady Letitia said with her usual accompanying sniff. Jeffrey never knew if that signified approval or not.

"It is my pleasure. Alessandra is shopping with her mother and her sister today, so I thought it might be nice to come calling." Even as he gave his explanation for the unanticipated visit, a picture of Alessandra's face looking up at him so hesitantly as she offered to cancel her plans for his sake, caused a stab of unreasonable vexation, which in turn caused him to quickly push aside the feeling and try to focus on the conversation at hand.

"Oh, it is so nice you've come," Jacqueline chimed in, her face wreathed in smiles as she handed him a cup of tea.

"I believe the summer weather is beginning to come along," Lady Letitia said.

"It has been more pleasant during the day, but the nights are still cold," Jeffrey said, inadvertently thinking of that freezing monstrosity of a room where he spent his nights.

"Last Sunday's service was pleasant, don't you think? All those summer flowers. Though, did you notice, Father Ainsley seemed distracted."

"Did he? I didn't notice, but I did find the flowers to be very nice." He nearly yawned, but caught himself before the tactless act could be committed.

The Dowager Lady Bremcott came to her feet, causing Jeffrey to rise as well. "In fact, it is such a pleasant day that I would like to suggest we remove to the gardens," she said.

"That sounds delightful," Jeffrey said, though privately he thought it a bit cool to be sitting out of doors. Nevertheless, he had decided to come here, so it was his duty to be obliging. It was not the ladies' fault that he had just as suddenly changed his mind and wished he hadn't come.

They sat on the tilted patio for a while, surveying the splendor of the gardens rich with flowers and engaging in desultory conversation, until a servant came to tell the elder Lady Bremcott she had another visitor. She reached to accept the calling card that the butler must surely have carried in to her.

"The lady said she was out of cards, my lady. She bid me ask you to indulge an old acquaintance," the butler said with a well-trained servant's careful lack of intonation in his voice.

"Why don't you two children take a stroll while I see who has come to call?" she suggested, rising from her whitewashed garden chair even as she wondered who would call without presenting a card.

Jeffrey, with an internal shrug, offered an arm to Jacqueline, who said, "I must show you Mother's prize-winning peonies." She led the way, at a very leisurely pace, down the steps and into the paved gardens, chattering brightly and smiling often, careful to avoid making any untoward remarks.

It was not until he had started to relax and enjoy her ambling conversation a little, that he realized that he had been rather glad of the Dowager Lady Bremcott's presence, wanting rather to avoid any more of those too-private, too-knowing conversations with Jacqueline. But now she was being her old self, quite charming, very pretty, sparkling even, no hint of persuasion in her tone, except perhaps for the tinkling laugh that invited him to enjoy the latest bon mot. He started to come away from his own thoughts and began to respond to her banter, letting her entertain him as she guided him through the garden paths.

Inside the house, the butler intoned, "Lady Jane Chenmarth." Having done his duty, he stepped aside from the parlor door to let the lady enter.

"Jane Chenmarth, what brings you to this end of town?" Lady Letitia greeted her in a welcoming, if not exactly friendly, manner.

"Did I see my son's chaise out front?" was her only reply as she glided into the room, pulling off her gloves.

"You did. He is strolling the gardens as we speak, with Jacqueline, of course."

"They are why I came here." Lady Jane's expression did not change, except for her eyes, which narrowed. "I was wondering if any apologies needed to be made."

"Am I to presume you are referring to the fact that Lord Huntingsley married that Hamilton girl?" Lady Letitia asked archly.

Lady Jane nodded briefly.

"My daughter explained why that had to be."

"Am I correct in assuming that this is something better left out of the social banter?"

"You assume correctly."

Lady Jane sat down, uninvited, slapping her gloves

against her hand, and said, "Ah then! So there is still some hope in this quarter that the Bremcotts and the Huntingsleys may unite some day."

"There is," Lady Letitia said, her face becoming a little pinched at the indelicacy of the topic, nonetheless glad that Lady Chenmarth had brought it up.

"This is what I wanted to know." Although Jane had just sat down, now she stood and crossed to the open doors that led out to the patio. A quick glance out into the gardens showed her where her son stood, though Jacqueline was too short to be seen over the hedge. It was clear, however, that her son was in the process of kissing the girl, if she was any judge of what his disappearance from sight for a full five seconds meant. She frowned to herself, but then shook her shoulders as though to dispel the sudden, unexpected reservation from her features before her hostess could note it. "Hmmm," she said to herself, turning from the doorway. "I am happy to see how open-minded you are being about all this."

"We must all try to be so, don't you think?"

"Indeed. But I confess I never would have pegged you as the kind to approve of a second marriage for your daughter."

"Oh, but it isn't really that, is it? I mean, he will have all his monies, estates, and no prior heirs. It will be as if he had never been married, surely?"

"Yes, that is a good way to look at it," Lady Jane said, slapping her hand once again with the gloves, as if to put an end to the matter.

But Lady Letitia was not finished. "I do hope you and your husband, and of course Lord Jeffrey himself, mean to handle this ending of the marriage with a quiet grace.

179

The sooner it is forgotten, the better for my girl."

"Of course. And I believe that Lady Amelia told me that they may be taking Alessandra out to the country for awhile. Lord Richard thinks this might not be such a bad idea for Jeffrey to do as well."

"Do you think there is going to be a scandal?" Letitia said, her hand fluttering up to her throat. "Jacqueline never thought there would be so much as a few tiny murmurs. . . ."

"No, no, there needn't be, need there? Since we are all in agreement, and I believe I speak for Jeffrey as I just saw him kissing your daughter behind the yew hedge, I see no reason why a second . . . *another* marriage cannot go forward in, say, a year or so from now," she said in her usual calm, straightforward fashion.

"A year," Lady Letitia murmured, moving toward the doors, peering agitatedly out into the garden. "She'll be twenty in a year."

"Don't bother to call them in. I'll see Jeffrey later. Leave them to enjoy their little stroll. We'll be in touch, I am sure, Lady Bremcott. Until then," she said, slipping her gloves back on, and leaving as unceremoniously as she had arrived.

Lady Letitia moved out into the garden, and found the young couple strolling, her daughter's head resting lightly against Jeffrey's shoulder as they moved.

"Lady Bremcott, I must be going now, but I wanted to thank you for the tea and the company," Jeffrey said as they spotted her.

"My pleasure, I'm sure," she replied, trying to organize her face to reflect none of the turmoiling emotions she was experiencing.

Jacqueline saw him to the door, then turned to find her mother had collapsed onto a settee and was waving an ornate vinaigrette box under her nose.

"What is it, Mother? Who came to call? Is there bad news?" she cried, running to her mother's side.

"It was Jeffrey's mother, Lady Jane, she was here. She wanted to check with me to see if our prior understanding was still in place, but now, my girl, I am not so certain that is such a good idea," she cried, distraught.

"Whyever not?" Jacqueline pulled back a little, affronted.

"I believe some people may look upon you as . . . as the *second wife!*" her mother cried.

Jacqueline frowned. "It is not the same as being 'the other woman,' you know, Mother."

"Oh, I am not so sure! It doesn't sound right. It sounds like the perfect material with which some of the nastier wits will make sport!"

"We cannot let such considerations guide us, Mother," Jacqueline said, but total conviction was lacking in her voice.

She helped her mother to sit upright, but as Lady Letitia fanned herself, her daughter began to wonder about the kiss she had just shared with Jeffrey Huntingsley.

She had been feeling triumphant at the eager way he had held her in his arms, his kiss at first restrained but then turning into a passionate insistence. She had thought this meant he was at last recognizing her worth. Perhaps he had not cared to see her situated so comfortably up on the Viscount Aldegard's phaeton at the park yesterday. Maybe he was at last aware that a young

181

girl would not be put off forever with vague words and lackluster pledges.

Now she wondered: had that kiss been the interest of a to-be husband, or had it been something else? Hadn't he lived with a wife who was no wife for a month now? Was he merely stealing kisses for the sake of pleasure? And why had the kiss ended abruptly, almost as if someone had stepped between them?

What had he said, anything? She thought she had murmured something about how "her only desire would be to make time fly," but had he said anything in return? Anything encouraging or promising? She frowned, trying to remember, and she thought perhaps he had only looked down at her, saying nothing. Nothing at all. No endearments, no reassurances. No, that was not quite true; he had said he must leave soon, because he was expected home at the dinner hour. She had thought nothing of it, but now . . . *home?* . . . what a strange kiss that had been! One moment it was gratifying and thrilling, his hands so firm on her arms, and the next it was as if he had suddenly removed himself. . . .

Oh, yes, of course! How silly of her to not think of it right away: he must have thought he was offending her sensibilities. *He probably thought he was the first man to ever kiss me,* she thought with an internal laugh. *He had not wanted to frighten me with ungentlemanly behavior.*

It was good that he had stopped, for she might have shown him otherwise if he had not.

"Don't worry, Mother. You know me. Jeffrey is always a one to play games, but he will treat me seriously enough, soon enough," Jacqueline said, smiling outwardly now.

"Don't be so sure, missy! I think we must consider all future plans with great caution."

Once again her mother caused her to frown with uncertainty. "That would not be unwise," she said at length. A mental picture of the Viscount Aldegard, smiling down at her with such enraptured concentration that he had almost dropped his leading lines, suddenly sprang unbidden to mind.

Chapter 15

"I don't feel like cribbage tonight," Jeffrey said to Alessandra the next evening when she came into the room. He had turned in his chair at the desk in their room, his face lost to shadows, for three lamps were placed behind him on the desk, unable to illuminate his features from behind. "I've been working on this model, if that is all right with you?"

"Oh, that's fine," she said, mildly surprised. They had only missed at playing cribbage two other nights, but both of those had been when Jeffrey and her father had closeted themselves with several bottles of port in the library. "I'll just read for awhile then," she said, crossing to the nighttable on her side of the bed and gathering up a romance that was not really very interesting.

It had been a good day, very enjoyable. Jeffrey had taken her to see an experimental museum—the most experimental part being that the exhibits moved from town to town, on gypsy-style wagons—and he had bought her lunch at a fashionable hotel, complete with ices for dessert. Then he had taken her for a round through the park, this time at the fashionable hour. There had been several acquaintances there who had claimed to have been sorely disappointed that they had not repeated the lovely picnic idea, making her laugh and promise to do so again sometime soon. She had relished being out and about, enjoying the outing almost as much as the one to St. Paul's, and the prior one at Green Park, that breathtaking day when he had tied her hat on for her. . . . The fresh air today, the pleasant company—Jeffrey had been most gallant, and had introduced her to several socially esteemed matrons—and left her feeling a happy, not too closely examined, glow.

She picked up a lamp and carried it over to where he was working. "May I have a light?" she asked, setting the lamp down and steadying it.

He reached for a rush and stuck it down the chimney of one of his lamps until it burst into flame, then he pulled it out and lowered it to the wick in her lamp.

"Thank you."

"You're welcome."

"Oh! I see you are working on a model of a ship."

"Yes, and do you see this?" he said, leaning back and reaching for a glass bottle.

"A ship in a bottle! I remember: Uncle Richie always tinkered on such projects. He must have shown you how to do it."

"After a certain someone tattled on me when I destroyed his."

She laughed, not at all chastised. "You'll have to pardon me for that, as I was only five. Five year olds generally are tattlemongers, you know. But, however does one get it in the bottle?"

"You see these masts? They can be collapsed, if

you are very steady of hand, and very clever—as am I, of course. You slide the collapsed model into the bottle with a string attached, settle it, then pull the masts aright."

"Have you ever spoiled one?" she asked, peering down at the tiny replication of a full-masted frigate that was nearing completion, amused by his self-given compliments.

"Not when it came to the sliding and setting of the sails aright, but I have a terrible time carving things the way I wish them. Only see this porthole on this one side: it's not even with the rest. I thought I had it, but it's not quite right, is it?" He pointed to the starboard porthole nearest the stern.

"Oh, but I don't know . . . it appears to me that you followed the line of the ship. Isn't that how it ought to be?"

He stared at it and grunted, and turned to the picture in the book spread out on his desk, comparing back and forth. "I'm not sure about it. I'll need to find another picture, from another angle."

"What is this?" she asked, pulling up a chair, her book forgotten on the dresser next to the desk. She held up a small, sharp object.

"Carving tool. Tiny, for this very kind of work, you see. Careful, it's sharp."

"How do you make the masts? They are so perfect. I would think one slip of the knife, and that would be the end of your mast."

He leaned back, his cupped hand sweeping a pile of broken, shredded sticks to where she could see them on the desk.

She laughed, and he joined her, their laughter ringing out to disturb the deep silence of the settled household.

187

"Do you know, you could be of some help to me," he said, wiping a sleeve across his eye to remove the tears that had formed there while he laughed.

"Could I? How? I should love to be of help," she said eagerly.

"I've no one to model my figurehead after. For you see, the 'lady' they chose for the illustration on this ship is a far sight from being what I would choose for mine. Would you pose for it?" He pointed to the place it would need to be on the bow of the ship.

Her eyes widened. "I? To be immortalized in wood? I should say I would like to do it," she said happily. She ought not to be so thrilled, she knew, for the figurehead pictured in the drawing of the ship was more of a tavern wench than a great beauty, but she could not care about that, for even if it was in just a small measure he had signified that he thought she was pretty enough to grace a ship. His ship.

"Is now too soon?"

"No, not at all," she said, a ripple of pleasure going through her at the thought.

"But I thought you were going to read . . . ?"

"Pooh. I can do that anytime. How is this?" she asked, striking a pose.

"Hmm. No, it needs to be more exaggerated." He stood, towering over her as he reached to put one hand on her chin, another on her back.

A shock ran through her at his touch, so that she almost pulled away. She flicked him a glance from the corner of her eyes as he gently lifted her chin a little farther.

"You should look as though you are scanning both the horizon and the heavens at once, seeking to avoid any dangers for your gallant crew," he said, enjoying the diversion they had made for themselves. He pressed with the flat of his hand, forcing her back to become more sloped, her breasts thrust forward in the classic design of the figurehead. "Yes, very nice," he said, and then wondered why he did not take his hands away at once. Instead they lingered there, almost as if of their own accord. Then he noticed that her mouth was not so very far from his own, that all he had to do was to bend a little to kiss her. It was a sweet mouth, both lips full and pink, slightly parted as she breathed from her unnatural positioning.

She saw something in his eyes, and though she had not seen it before, though she did not have an experienced woman's insight, her heart began to skitter around her rib cage almost painfully.

He started to bend down to her, not really hearing his own alarms sounding, his eyes intent on that luscious, slightly trembling bow of a mouth. Of their own volition, his eyes went on, to travel up to meet her own eyes. Eyes full of wonderment and disturbance, as brightly blue as . . . as . . .

He blinked, and straightened himself again slowly, and sluggishly recalled that it was Lord Malcolm Hamilton who also had such vivid blue eyes. And it was Lord Malcolm who would laugh if the annulment could not go forward.

A kiss, the kiss, that had seemed but a moment ago so right, now was seen clearly once again as a dangerous thing. His hands, those that had been ready to caress her, now fell from her woodenly.

He turned brusquely away, blindly seizing up the ship's model and one of his carving tools. The tool slipped through his nerveless fingers, slicing the middle one as it passed through to clatter on to the floor. "Demme!" he cried, thrusting the injured finger into his mouth.

"Are you all right?" she cried, rising shakily. She had to take a deep breath to steady herself, then she went to the basin, and immediately brought back a wet cloth, which she handed to him. "Shall I get bandages?"

"Yes, please, though something small would be sufficient, I think," he answered, wrapping the wet cloth around the offended finger. He wondered somewhat wildly if she could see the pulse he could feel pounding through the vein at his temple.

She left, taking up her lamp, hurrying downstairs to the antechamber that led the way out to the separate laundry building. Patty had several kinds and sizes of cloth bandages there, making quick work for Alessandra. Grabbing up a pair of scissors and Mama's own specially prepared ointment, she was back upstairs in but a few minutes.

It was short work to fashion a bandage around his finger.

"Sorry," he said, having had time to regain his equanimity. "No carving for me tonight, eh?" he said, laughing briefly.

"I should say not."

It would have been an easy thing then to take a moment and discourage the using of her for his figure-head's model, or at least to say nothing of it at all, but he found his mouth speaking without apparent connection to his brain. "Will you pose for me later? In a few days, when this cut is healed?"

"Of course," she said, but she would not meet his eyes.

He reached down to the floor, retrieving his carving

implement and setting it in its place in the case with the others. He closed the wooden lid, then looked up at her where she still stood close to him, presumably checking to see if he was going to bleed through the bandage. "I think I'll go to the library, to see if Lord Malcolm has any other pictures of frigates to be found there."

"Very well. I am going to read in bed for a while," she said, then blushed a little, thinking that had sounded somehow terribly suggestive, as though she meant to wait up for him. She had not meant it to sound that way.

"I may be gone some time."

"I'll leave a lamp burning for you."

"Thank you," he said, standing. She moved away, avoiding contact.

"You're welcome. I'll say good night then, in case I am not awake when you come up."

"Good night."

She dressed in her nightclothes slowly, not in her usual dash-about style, when he had left. For a moment she had been sure they were going to kiss.

He had recalled himself—that she understood easily; what troubled her was why he had meant to kiss her in the first place? He did not love her; he did not want her for a wife.

She furrowed her brow, trying to decipher between Emmeline and Mama's recitals of men's appetites to see where an explanation might lie. Was he prey to the same kind of heated blood that ran through her body, that she was even more acutely aware of when they had been dancing together, making her unrealistic and nonsensical? It had seemed to make her dizzy, and for a fact had never lent itself to the practice of clear thinking. Did men feel that way, too? Didn't Mama try to tell her men had to have certain things, certain ways? This would have been just a kiss, yet didn't kisses lead to . . . that other? But no, not necessarily, surely not. Maybe Jeffrey just liked kissing. *No, he drew back . . . but he almost kissed me . . . he doesn't want me . . . but he likes me, I know he does, I know it . . .* Her thoughts tumbled on and on, the book lying forgotten where it lay across her chest as she stared restlessly out from the emptiness of the bed into the darkness of the silent night.

When he came up to bed, his candle guttering in its stick as he walked as quietly as he could across the marbled floor, he saw that the lamp on his side of the bed was flickering and about to die out, and that Alessandra's already had. Her book rested face down across her nightgown-covered breasts, and her long braid of dark hair had escaped to fall over the edge of the bed. Her face, already so young in appearance, was even more so in repose.

He watched the book rise and fall as she breathed, and reached to carefully remove it, setting it aside on the nighttable. He bent to lift her long braid, caressing its silky texture for a moment before he settled it on the bed along the lie of her arm above the covers. That her arm, clothed in spun cotton, was outside the covers and her head uncovered by its usual cap was an indication that the nights were finally starting to warm up a bit, and he recognized a pang of regret when he wondered how long it would be before he would be sleeping on the floor. Perhaps she would allow him to remain, for a bed was ever so much more comfortable than the floor.

He resolved not to broach the subject unless she did.

He reached up to rub his tired eyes, then bent and blew out the candle he had set on her nighttable. He crossed to his side of the bed, and blew out that lamp as well. The moon was bright, shining through the one window where the curtains had not been closed for the evening.

Since it was obvious that she was sleeping, he undressed there in the room, smiling ever so slightly at the thought of how scandalized she would be were she to wake. He almost kind of, sort of, wished that she would, if just to see those blue eyes open wide in bemusement to find him disrobing in her presence.

When he was clothed in his nightshirt, he crawled into bed. He saw that she was still sleeping, so he stretched over the pillow, kissed the tip of his own forefinger, and placed it very gently against her lips. *There,* he told himself, *now I have kissed her, and I needn't think about it anymore.*

Chapter 16

"I don't think you should go."

"Nonsense, Mother. Why, we are practically engaged," Jacqueline reproved, her green eyes bright.

"You are hardly that, not when he has a wife!"

"I am when he kisses me in gardens," she concluded in a sweetened voice that nonetheless demanded no further arguments from her mother.

"You will be back here at four! I won't have that nice Lord Aldegard making his horses wait."

"I'll be back before then, you may be sure, for I will want to change," Jacqueline said calmly.

"Be sure that Mrs. Adams stays with you. *Every minute.*"

Jacqueline just shook her head mildly, noting with mild irritation that her companion, Mrs. Adams, looked, in her disapproval of the proposed visit, even more like a worried hedgehog than she usually did.

Jacqueline was greeted at the front door of New Garden Hall by Mr. Cloch. "Lord and Lady Huntingsley are not at home. Do you care to leave a card, my lady?"

Mr. Cloch asked of the caller.

"When will they be back?"

Mr. Cloch's first response was a moment of stunned silence, and Mrs. Adams actually gasped in something like horror, for such a question was certainly presumptuous, at best. His second was to recall that Lady Bremcott had been a caller many times, and might therefore be forgiven for a small social lapse in the face of friendship and long-standing acquaintance. "I should think Lord and Lady Huntingsley would be returning shortly, my lady," Mr. Cloch said austerely.

"I will wait," Jacqueline answered firmly, sweeping in through the door, not waiting to be invited in.

The butler caught Mrs. Adams's shocked eye, but then inclined his head, and led the ladies to the front parlor to wait. When he left them, he did not order a tea tray sent in, sagely waiting to see if the master desired to entertain these unexpected guests.

"I did not!" a female voice floated into the room a minute later, preceding Alessandra's entrance.

Jacqueline saw her first, out in the hallway that led to the parlor. She noted at once that Alessandra's hair was beginning to tumble down, her hat was slightly askew, and she was hobbling.

"You did so cheat, and that is why you were thrown," Jeffrey replied, helping her falter her way along. "Gracie will stand for none of that kind of behavior."

Jacqueline saw that laughing lights danced in his eyes, and that his coat was covered with dusty smears, as well as his boots. His one arm was under Alessandra's, the other around her shoulders, holding her up with the embrace.

All at once Alessandra spotted Jacqueline, just as Mr. Cloch reappeared and belatedly announced, "My Lord! My Lady! Uh, Lady Jacqueline Bremcott has come to call."

"So we see," Jeffrey said, coming to a halt. "Could you send for tea, please, Cloch?"

"Yes, my lord."

Jeffrey then continued to assist Alessandra into the parlor, and onto a settee, from which she greeted their guest. "Lady Bremcott. How nice to see you again." If her voice sounded a little hollow, it could easily be explained by the fact that her ankle was in pain.

Jacqueline was well versed in good manners. She murmured, "Have I come at a bad time? Should I return later?" but the question was addressed to Jeffrey, whose back was mostly turned to her. He was lifting Alessandra's foot, settling it atop a footstool, placing one of the sofa cushions under it.

Finally he turned, and replied, "Of course not. Cook would be furious if I sent for tea and no one stayed to consume any of it."

Jacqueline almost frowned, for the comment seemed vaguely unwelcoming. Of course, he could hardly be warm and affectionate with his wife—if such she could be called—sitting right there. Jacqueline turned and motioned her companion forward, introducing her, "This is Mrs. Adams."

Jeffrey nodded to her, and said, "Of course. We've met before, Mrs. Adams." Then, with a wave toward the chairs, he said, "Ladies, please, won't you have a seat?"

Jacqueline settled on the edge of the proffered chair, knowing that in every way she must surely appear more at advantage than Alessandra, who was lounging back, her foot up, her skirts being crushed under her as she did so. "Your hat, it is falling to one side," she told her hostess in the most helpful tone.

"Is it? So it is," Alessandra replied, reaching up to undo the pins that held it in place. When she pulled off the hat, her hair was made all the more mussed. She felt a faint flush creep into her face, and hoped it would be ascribed to pain rather than embarrassment. What did she have to compare with this green-eyed beauty? Why should she even care that her unfashionably long hair was mussed? It was not as if she had any reason to think Jeffrey would care to look at her or her appearance, not with any real attention, not so long as the cool and lovely Lady Bremcott was in the room.

So thinking, she defiantly pulled the rest of the pins from her hair, allowing it to tumble down around her shoulders unhampered. "Excuse me," she said coolly, with a sudden need to form an excuse, "but I think I must rest. I find I have a bit of a headache since I lost my seat on Gracie."

"Do you?" Jeffrey asked, coming to his feet at once. "I did not think! Allow me to take you upstairs. Of course we must have Patty see to your headache, as well as your ankle. Excuse us, please, ladies. I will return shortly, after I see that Alessandra is made comfortable."

So saying, he bent and scooped her up into his arms. She was tiny, weighing almost nothing it seemed, as he carried her toward the stairs. Jacqueline looked on, her green eyes snapping emerald fire when she saw the other woman's hair spreading out over Jeffrey's arm like a dark, gossamer fan. The girl pressed her pretty face close to Jeffrey's waistcoat, her sky blue eyes looking up with something shy and yet covertly possessive about them.

Jacqueline would have been further disconcerted if she had known that Alessandra's heart was swelling with joy that Jeffrey was attending her so well, even if, as she could only assume, it was only out of good manners. Her delicate hands held on to his lapels as if she would hold on to him and not allow him to return to the parlor without her, even if she pretended she did it so as not to fall from his grasp.

Emmeline had come to the top of the stairs. She looked at them quizzically as Jeffrey came up toward her, her sister in his arms. A quick explanation was enough to bring Emmeline along to the Sapphire Room to assist.

It was a full half-hour before Jeffrey returned to the parlor, apologizing for the delay. "Alessandra sends her regrets. It was not such a nasty fall, but it is better she rest. I have been teasing her that it was her fault that she was thrown, but in truth I think Beast must have tried to take a nip out of Gracie."

"Beast?" Jacqueline said, her tone as cold as the tea now was in her cup.

"My horse. He's always been called just 'Beast,' because it suits his bad temper, as is demonstrated once again by this little accident."

"Why don't you get a different horse?" Jacqueline asked, growing weary of the topic already.

"Give up Beast? No, he'll be around until he's put out to pasture."

"Jeffrey," she cut across his conversation abruptly, "Could you show me the gardens?"

He looked puzzled, and said, "But it rained last night."

"I don't mind. I'm prepared with my half boots, so a little wet grass won't bother a thing." She lifted a corner of her skirts, revealing the boots so mentioned. At the risqué move, Jeffrey and Mrs. Adams exchanged quick glances, the one startled, the other stunned.

"Very well," he said, standing, smoothing out his rumpled coat with one hand, even as he strove to smooth over Jacqueline's blatant coquettishness for her chaperone's sake. He belatedly recalled that he was dirty and dusty. *Oh well, why change before going out into a wet garden?* he thought with mild irritation.

"Mrs. Adams, I would like you to stay here to direct the servants to bring more hot tea," Jacqueline said over her shoulder to that lady, even as her hand reached to unlatch the door to the garden.

Mrs. Adams twisted her hands together worriedly, unable to contain her expressions as well as her tongue, but she stayed behind, murmuring protests against being parted from the company of her charge.

Jacqueline was not in the best of humors, having had to sit and wait for Jeffrey's company while he tended to another woman. Therefore, questions that she would have known better than to ask had she felt less miffed, came forth. "So how long does it take to get this annulment over with?"

"Jacqueline—"

"I spoke discreetly to an old classmate of mine, and she believes that this can take a *year* or better!" she agitated.

He cast her a dark glance, and said, "I suppose it could. The bishop, from all signs that I've seen, does not care to move rapidly on the matter. I'm not even sure that he has any such authority to do so."

"Well, why don't you find out?"

"Don't you think I have been trying to do just that?" he snapped. Then he sighed discontentedly, and said, "I suppose I shall have to go see the man myself. This vicar is not a very effective fellow."

"That sounds like a good plan."

"I'm glad you agree." If she noticed the sarcasm in his voice, she did not acknowledge it. Honestly, she was as bad about hounding a person as Elias sometimes was; sarcasm was often lost on his brother as well, though one had to say in general that Elias was at least a little more convivial when enacting his provocations.

"Jeffrey, I have your handkerchief to return to you," she said, the irritation dropping away and being replaced by a honeyed tone. She produced the cloth she had borrowed so long ago, on which to dry her tears when first he had told her that he was to marry Alessandra.

He accepted the bit of fabric, and something caught his eye. She had stitched their initials on one corner: JH— JB. He scowled at the initials, then jammed it in his coat pocket, saying nothing to her. She was wise enough to cozen on to the fact that it would be better if she said nothing further of it to him as well.

If she had hoped for another kiss in the garden, she was bound to be disappointed. The moment did not arise, as they were both out of sorts with each other. Jeffrey looked up toward the windows that showed into the Sapphire Room, knowing Alessandra could not be at the window, but he had a faintly disturbed feeling anyway, as if eyes were watching him.

Emmeline looked down past the sapphire velvet curtains, being careful to stay to one side, out of sight. There was certainly nothing loverlike in the posture of the two below; if anything, they looked rather as if they were quarreling. Still, Elias had said something about Jeffrey marrying "that stick Jacqueline Bremcott." And Emmeline had caught a glimpse of the look on Jacqueline's face as Jeffrey carried Alessandra up the stairs. The girl had been more than a little annoyed. Elias must be right: the Lady Jacqueline bore watching . . . as did the shyly admiring glances that Alessandra had given Jeffrey as he had borne her up the stairs.

Emmeline crossed to the bed where her sister should have been fussing and complaining about her injured ankle, but all she found was Alessandra, her head in the clouds, humming a happy tune lightly. "Should we send for a doctor?" Emmy asked dubiously.

"No, Patty set me all to rights. Why are you frowning at me so?" Alessandra asked, the bandaged foot still but the other one beating out the rhythm of the song she immediately went back to humming.

"I have morning sickness," Emmeline hedged a half-truth.

"Well then, lie down beside me and we shall convalesce together," Alessandra said, cheerfully patting the bed beside her. "When are you going home to James?" she asked, when her sister had settled beside her.

"He's due back from Brussels at the end of the month. Alessandra," she said seriously, "if you should ever want to come stay with us, you would be most welcome."

"How very kind. I shall do that sometime."

"Do you think you would come soon?"

"Oh, I can't. Papa is making Jeffrey and I stay here

202

until the annulment."

"And after that?" Emmeline asked carefully.

Alessandra's merriment fell away, and she frowned at her bandaged foot thoughtfully. "Of course, I'll come then, probably when your baby is born."

"But what if the annulment is not in place by then?"

"Oh, well then, I don't think Papa would keep me here, not with his first grandchild to consider, and not with mama coming along, naturally. Perhaps we'll all come, and make your home into bedlam until you throw us all out."

"Jeffrey, too?"

"I . . . I suppose," Alessandra said uncertainly, a shadow crossing over her face.

Emmeline closed her eyes, willing the little touch of morning sickness away, and also willing all her sister's troubles could be settled long before the baby arrived. Though, even to herself, she had to admit that the exact nature of the term "settled" escaped her, try as she might to see what would be best for this relationship.

Emmeline was still reclining at her sister's side when Jeffrey returned. He looked momentarily surprised to find someone else in the chambers, but swiftly went on to announce, "Our guests have gone. Jacqueline tells me that her mother is planning a formal ball soon."

"Not too soon, I hope, or I would not be able to dance," Alessandra said, indicating her ankle, the prospect of not being able to dance with Jeffrey—while others could—making a spot in the middle of her chest ache rather abominably.

"We'll know when we get the invitation, but I assume it could not be so soon as to be a worry. You know that Lady Letitia likes to do everything correctly. And speaking of correctly, should we send for the doctor?" he asked, reaching out a hand to examine the bandaging that held her ankle stiffly.

"No. Patty has done her best by me. She said it was a fairly bad sprain, and that I was not to walk on it for a few days if I can help it, but that is all. I trust her opinion. We needn't bother the doctor."

"I see everyone is in here," Lady Amelia called from the doorway, just removing her poke hat from coming inside.

"Mama, you're home."

"Whatever happened?" that lady cried, coming into the room to see the bandaging up close.

"Gracie threw me, and I hurt my ankle. I'm very proud of myself, though, for I did, however poorly, manage to land on my feet and not my head," Alessandra said with the dimple coming to her cheek.

"An excellent horsewoman," Jeffrey agreed, and she was gratified to hear that he sounded quite sincere.

"Should we send for the doctor?"

"No!" all three of the young people said at once.

They all laughed together, and Alessandra had to explain to her mother that the question had been asked and answered twice already.

"Where is Papa? I thought you two had gone to look at new furnishings together," Emmeline said.

"He went on to Tattersall's, speaking of horses. As if this household needs another horse!"

"Another one for Beast to take a nip out of," Jeffrey agreed.

"Beast holds nothing over Malcolm Huntingsley when it comes to snippiness. Honestly, that man has the most backward of tastes! Egyptian, that's what he wanted. But it is so passé!"

They fell into conversation, and before long a game of whist was being played across the surface of the bed.

Quite unlike a wounded patient, Alessandra's face was aglow, her part in the discourse as bright and bubbly as her smile. Emmeline, however, was uncharacteristically quiet and observant.

Jeffrey awoke to a loud thump. He sat up in bed, looking over the pillow and seeing at once that Alessandra was not in her place. "Alessandra?" he whispered loudly into the gloom.

It was silent for a moment, but then she answered, "Here. On the floor."

"What are you doing on the floor?" he asked, as he crawled out from under the covers.

"I slipped."

"Your ankle!"

"Exactly."

"Well, what were you trying to do?" he asked, coming around the bed and stooping in front of her. She caught a flash of skin up to his thigh, and averted her eyes.

"I was trying to get to the necessary," she said through gritted teeth.

"Oh. Well. Let me help you then." He gathered her up into his arms, staggering for just a second, searching for purchase. In a moment he was steadied, and he carried her to the dressing room, kicking the door aside as he passed through. He set her down near the convenience, and backed out of the room, saying, "Call me when you're ready."

He rubbed his hands up and down his arms, hopping from one foot to the other to try to stave off some of the early morning chill as he waited.

Time elapsed, and she did not signal, so he called out, "Are you all right?"

"I . . . I have a problem. Can you ring for Patty?"

"Alessandra, it's three in the morning!"

She was silent, so finally he said, "Can't I help you?"

"No!" she cried.

"What do you need?"

"Supplies."

"Supplies?"

"Female supplies."

He was starting to become irritated, then suddenly he understood and felt abashed. "Right. I'll just ring for Patty."

The maid came to their room, her clothes hastily thrown on, her look sour. He gave her to understand that her mistress was in the dressing room, and then crawled back into bed. "Well," he said softly to himself, "every servant will know by morning that there's no Huntingsley heir on its way soon."

He crossed his arms behind his head, gazing sightlessly up at the ceiling, realizing he had not given much real thought to having an heir. It was something that was supposed to come one day, like marrying Jacqueline. An heir. His heir. His child.

Strange how the thought of begetting a successor could send this tingle of promise through a man's spirit, how it could make him think of himself and his life and

206

his future. That was natural, of course, but still there was something distinctly stirring about the very thought.

Oh yes, he was definitely coming to that point in life that parents referred to as "settling down," and he could see that there was something to the idea. Children, his own, making his life noisy and full of bother, their dark hair . . . no, no, make that *blond* curls gleaming in the sun as they played on the lawns of . . . where? Perhaps he could move back to Huntingsley Hall? That made a pleasant picture for his mind's eye, though he could just as easily imagine finding his own home, a place to start anew.

Patty came from the dressing room, her mistress's arms draped over her shoulders as they hobbled forward together. She helped Alessandra into bed, her sour look having faded to a rather maternal clucking, and if she noticed the oddly placed pillow between them, it did not register on her kindly face.

When she had gone, they were silent, quite aware that the other was awake. At length, Alessandra said, "I am so mortified."

"But why?" he asked, sincerely baffled. "It's normal."

"Not between us, it's not."

He had nothing to say to that, feeling strangely discontent at her faintly embittered words.

When he awoke in the morning, the extra pillow was under his head, he was on his stomach, and his right arm was lying along Alessandra's back. He lay there unmoving for a little while, observing the tiny sensations that went with touching someone else. There was the shared warmth; the softness of the fabric of her nightgown; the way small movements allowed him to feel each individual hair on his arm as it lay pressed against her; and the tickling of a long, loose, dark hair across his skin.

After a while, he slowly, carefully moved his arm, rolling to lie in the opposite direction, to pretend at being still asleep until she began to stir for the day.

They had worked out a system where they reported the next day's activities before retiring for the night, so that they could determine who should rise first. It was Alessandra's turn, and she reached for the bellpull. Angie came in time and helped her to the dressing room, coming back to the room to select articles of clothing, then disappearing back into the dressing room. Before long, Alessandra was helped back to one of the chairs before the fire. "I'll bring yer tray right quick," Angie whispered loudly.

Jeffrey opened his eyes, finding it awkward to pretend to be sleeping when he was not, and found Alessandra looking directly at him. She flushed a little, and murmured, "Good morning."

"Good morning." He stretched under the covers, and gave a big yawn.

"Are we still going to London Tower today?"

"Yes, I planned on it."

"At two? I promised Emmeline that I would help her start to let out some of her gowns this morning."

"Two is fine." He sat up, the front of his nightshirt parting open almost down to his navel. The tie must have come undone some time last night. He reached to retie it, pretty sure Alessandra had noticed, for she was blushing and looking away.

It was Patty who returned with the tray, setting it on the little table they usually used for cribbage and which

208

Angie had placed before her mistress, as she explained, "Angie's helping Cook, my lady, so I said as I'd bring this up ta yer."

Jeffrey lay back on the pillows, pondering whether or not he was expected to wait until she had eaten before he could get out of bed. *I will not,* he thought in mild defiance of this unspoken portion of their "contract," and reached for the bellpull. Winters came in shortly after, and though he must have been a little surprised to find Alessandra there, without raising so much as an eyebrow, nodded a greeting to her and bid her good morning.

"I wish to wear dark gray today," Jeffrey told his man. "I am going back to Pithers, Ostrum, and Williams today, and wish to look suitably clerkish."

"Very good, my lord," Winters replied, moving to start gathering his master's ensemble together.

"You plan to work on the estate matters?" Alessandra asked as she buttered a scone.

"'Tis why I was sent to London in the first place. I must say, I believe my father was correct in saying that the barristers would find my estate records a different matter than I do. Penny wise and pound foolish, as the saying goes."

"Why is that?"

"Oh, I suppose it's not their fault, being town fellows, but they had drafted up a five-year plan that included never allowing three of my father's fields to lie fallow, as if they could produce forever, season after season."

"Well, even I know better than that."

"So all those romps out to Timepiece Manor left their mark, did they?" he smiled at her approvingly.

"Timepiece. I had almost forgotten its name." Her

smile was soft and sweetened by memories of days in the country sun.

"All those clocks in the study."

"Yes, I remember they drove a person quite mad, with all their chiming and ding-donging, especially along about midnight."

"Now *I*," he said, throwing his legs over the side of the bed, for he saw that Winters was ready for him, "I remember loving to hear the clocks striking the midnight hour. Do you recall Cousin Roger? He and I would sneak out of the house, and down into the chapel, to see if anything untoward or spooky happened at the witching hour, but—alas!—but for our vivid imaginations, it never did."

"Cousin Roger. I'd almost forgotten him, too. He's on the Peninsula now, with the army, isn't he?"

"I believe so."

"I saw a ghost there once, at Timepiece Manor," Alessandra said.

He stood up and moved in front of her, crossing his arms across his chest. "No!" he cried with a wide dash of relish in his posture.

"I was sure I had, but Emmeline came down the hall with me, and ended up proving it was only Old Puss."

"That flea-bitten thing? How disappointing."

"At the time I was quite relieved." She smiled up at him, then said quietly, "May I say something . . . in private?" She cast a look toward Winters.

Jeffrey waved his man into the dressing room.

"Thank you for helping me last night," she said, turning her countenance toward the fire, unable to look at him.

210

"Of course." Spontaneously, without meaning to, he crossed the couple of feet to her side, and leaned down and planted a kiss on her cheek. If he had had any intention in mind, it had been to give her a family kiss, something that said "I like you, don't worry about it," but when his lips touched her smooth skin, something very like a spark leapt into his mouth, and he lingered longer than he ought to have done. As she started to pull away, he allowed his mouth to trail across hers, barely touching, as if in passing, and for a second he thought he felt her lips respond under his. No, he had imagined that, or he had just taken her by surprise, surely.

He stood up, mentally and physically shaking himself, pretending to be cold. He cleared his throat, and said huskily, "And if you are here in our room at two, I will carry you down to the carriage."

"I'm sure I could contrive a way to get down the stairs," she said, her voice very small.

"Why risk it? No, I'll meet you here."

She did not refuse him. "Anyway, thank you again. You have been very patient and very understanding."

He gazed down at her soberly, realizing he was not appropriately dressed for standing about and conversing, but not really caring. Why should a nightshirt be any the more shocking just because the sun was up? He wanted to thank her for the comments, wanted to compliment her in return, and he wanted to deny that anything had been all that much trouble, but he could not think of a way to say so simply and easily. Instead, he respected her remarks by merely nodding, then proceeded to the dressing room.

He watched his own reflection as he was being dressed,

211

assessing the head that common sense told him was finely shaped, the hair that needed a trim but was not unruly, the dark eyes set well above an aristocratic nose and cheekbones, and the handsome mouth with white, healthy teeth. He saw wide shoulders tapering to slim hips and a flat stomach that could only help to complement the lie of his inexpressibles and his waistcoat. He knew Winters enjoyed dressing him, that he relished that his master's long neck showed his well-tied cravats to advantage, and that his shapely calves filled out the silk stockings or pantaloons that were handwashed by the servant personally. Jeffrey knew he had strong, muscular legs, for he liked walking and enjoyed riding often, and his feet were neither too big nor too small. What he saw in his mirror told him again what he had always rather offhandedly known: that he was an attractive man, capable of sending a flutter through a maidenly breast or two.

The only thing that shocked him at all, as he stared into his own eyes, was the thought that he wondered why that maidenly flutter was not evinced by Alessandra. Why were her blushes all from embarrassment, and none from attraction? Why did she not kiss him back? Perhaps, for a second she had. . . . But why didn't she ever touch his hand, or push back the hair from his forehead, or read aloud to him . . . in bed. . . .

No, he did not want that! He must not let a desire to assuage his own vanity propel him toward any behavior that might encourage Alessandra to grow fond of him. He must remember, as his mother told him so urgently that day, that there was nothing worse than loving someone who did not love you back. It would be too cruel for

Alessandra, after all her goodness, if he flirted and played games that led her young heart toward hurt. Who was he to look for something that would only be most inappropriate in their circumstances? Get rid of such foolish meanderings of the mind, he told himself, glaring into his own eyes harshly. Leave well enough alone.

Winters left his master scowling at himself in the mirror, unable to solicit the reason for Lord Jeffrey's displeasure, and having to assume that neither he nor his efforts were at fault. He began to sort the previous day's clothing from around the room, placing several items from the pockets onto the dresser, not least of which was Lord Jeffrey's money purse. His mouth twitching with censure at the master's casualness, Winters made two separate bows to his lord and lady, and left with the appropriate garments with which he had to contend.

Jeffrey came back into the main room, pulling on his ear, obviously thinking about the day ahead. He idly gathered up his belongings. Among them he found once again the handkerchief that Jacqueline had embroidered. Without so much as a thought, he crumpled it up and tossed it in the waste bin, and stuffed the other items in the pockets of his jacket. "I'll be home before two," he told her. With a puzzled shake of his head, he observed to himself that he had called this ghastly room "home," but then it had been his sleeping place for well over a month now. "Shall I ring for Patty?" he asked.

"Please."

He did as she had bid, and then said, "I shall bear thee down anon, good lady." It was odd, he had not needed to say such a silly thing, but it had just come out of his mouth. Another silly little phrase, one that he knew

213

would make her smile, popped into his mind, but he firmly suppressed it, and promptly left, forbidding himself to stand about, lingering just because he had no particular place to go this morning.

Patty came, bearing away the tray and offering to return to help move Alessandra to a window seat in "two shakes of a lamb's tail."

The maid came back, helped Alessandra, and began straightening up the room. She returned to her mistress's side, holding the waste bin in one hand, and the handkerchief by two fingers in the other. "Yer don't care to throw this away, do yer?" she asked.

Jeffrey had thrown that kerchief away . . . how odd. Was it stained? Alessandra took it, and saw that it was not a stain that marked one side, but embroidery. Initials: JH—JB.

She nearly gasped, but then folded it unevenly, and looked up at Patty with something of a wild look in her eyes. "No, it's fine. I'll keep it."

"Yer don't want me ta wash it?"

"I'll put it in the laundry basket when I'm ready."

"And what about this riding 'abit of yers? I think a little soakin' wif my special solution might take th' dirt stains out."

"That sounds fine." She managed a thin smile. She could hardly wait until Patty was gone, which thankfully proved to be relatively soon. She then smoothed open the kerchief, staring at the initials again. Who else's initials could they be but Jeffrey Huntingsley's and Jacqueline Bremcott's? Especially coming from Jeffrey's pocket. *She,* that Jacqueline, had sewn this; *she* had put their initials together so possessively; that woman, that

214

creature, that one who would cherish another woman's husband—!

Her thoughts jerked forward toward thoughts even more harsh and less patient as she scolded herself: *Whose husband? You have to be a wife to have a husband. You are no wife. You'll never be his wife. Let her have him; they want each other. He doesn't want you, not even if he thinks he wants to try to kiss you, not even if his body sometimes presses close to yours for warmth, not even if he is gentlemanly, and courtly, and kind. Kindliness can be given to a dog, idly, so how can you think of yourself as being of any worth to him, of having any right to his fidelity? He is being honorable, leaving you free, so why are you fighting against what is surely best?* she chided herself, biting her lip until she could stand it no more, and began to weep.

"Lessie? Lessie, what's wrong?" Emmeline opened her door, and came flying across the room to her, the sobs having reached to her past the closed door as she passed by in the hallway.

Alessandra collapsed into her sister's arms, and sobbed out an erratic explanation, finally just handing the hated kerchief into Emmeline's hands as she sank onto her bed and cried into her pillow, a pillow that smelled faintly of soap and leather, of Jeffrey.

"You say you found it in the wastebasket?"

The dark head nodded on the pillow, her face smothered away from sight, her tears nearly spent.

"And Jeffrey put it there?"

Again a nod.

"Did he know you saw him do so?"

Alessandra lifted her tear-stained face and sniffed shakily until she could command her features enough to

215

look at her sister and say, "I guess so."

"Then why are you so upset? If he cared about the handkerchief, wouldn't he have placed it away somewhere, someplace private? Why would he throw it away, right in front of you? I don't understand why you are upset. Do you *want* him to admire Jacqueline Bremcott?"

Alessandra stared at her, her mouth slightly open in amazement. "I . . . I didn't think of it quite like that."

"So, you were upset because you thought that something special was going on between those two?" Emmeline moved to pull her sister to a sitting position, pulling the dark head to rest on her shoulder.

"Their fathers had an understanding. They were supposed to wed. He told me he talked to her, that she understood. I've seen them together. . . . I've made certain conclusions," she said hesitantly, starting to feel foolish, wondering once again what claim she had to make on Jeffrey's affections.

"Come now, love, let us think about this." It was on the tip of Emmeline's tongue to accuse Alessandra of having done exactly what she had tried to warn her that evening in the garden not to do: fall in love with Jeffrey. But she did not ask, not wanting to hear the answer, not wanting to believe the evidence all around her. "If it is true that Jeffrey means to wed Jacqueline, we must assume that they plan to marry quite some time later, after all the dust settles from the annulment, of course. You need not fear that people will talk about you in any connection with their subsequent marriage." She abruptly changed directions, saying, "Mama tells me that she is quite sure you would have several suitors, and she

216

is hopeful that we may not even have to leave London. I want you to stop fretting about whether Jeffrey is going to help us be discreet," she deliberately put a misunderstanding spin on Alessandra's tears, "and start concentrating on attracting other offers. I, and Mama, will help you. Oh, won't it be grand when you finally get to establish your own home and your own nursery? Perhaps my second baby and your first will be born around the same time; wouldn't that be lovely?"

She prattled on, thinking that she might have succeeded in distracting Alessandra from her misery.

She thought also, briefly, of Elias, who had asked her to keep her eye on her little sister and Jeffrey. She could not think he would be pleased to have her advising Lessie to think of other beaux, but what other course could there be? It seemed clear enough to Lessie, and to herself, that Jacqueline Bremcott had good reason to believe Jeffrey wished her for his wife. Yes, very clear.

Although, she thought to herself with a mental lifting of her eyebrows, sometimes very clear waters run much deeper than one ever would suspect, as her bookish, reserved, proper husband had taught her any number of times in the privacy of their bedchambers. Jeffrey had not placed the handkerchief under his pillow, or in his drawer, or his vest pocket—he had thrown it away. Perhaps the "obvious" course must be reevaluated, Emmeline mused as she cradled her disconsolate little sister.

Alessandra was very subdued when Jeffrey came at two to carry her down to the carriage. She had little to say, and they did not stay long at the Tower, each quickly finding their fill of interesting facts, or as in her case, pretending to.

As he carried her back up the stairs at home, she tried to think of some way to injure her ankle again—or perhaps she could contrive to break a leg?—anything that could insure that this physical closeness, however innocuous on his part, would continue.

Chapter 17

Across town, a heart, more matronly than maidenly, beat an unsteady tattoo as she poured out tea for her husband. "You came . . . to talk?" she asked shakily, one hand at the pulse that beat at her throat as she placed the tea offering on the low table before him.

"Yes, to talk," Lord Richard answered calmly, though his eyes were flashing. "Jeffrey came to see me. He said some strange things. Acted very odd, don't you know. I've come to see if you have any idea what is happening in that quarter."

She poured out a dish of tea for herself, her eyes lowered that he might not see the girlish eagerness that had suddenly overtaken her by his mere presence in her sitting room.

"He claims he wants an annulment," she said quietly.

"So he tells me, but . . . oh, I don't know! It doesn't sound right somehow, the way he says it. Distasteful business, all, but still he gets a rather pinched look about his face . . . have you noticed anything? I feel as though we ought to do something for them, help them out some way. Or am I being a silly, doddering old father?" he said in a bluster. He did not reach for his tea, not wanting her to see the way his hands trembled slightly. Heavens, but she was looking fine today, all decked out in a rich burgundy, her hair, lightly etched with silver, swept back into a languorous chignon. Her face, never in need of a rouge pot, was still as fine boned and attractive as ever. In fact, he rather liked the way the skin crinkled around her eyes, and the faint laugh lines that defined her mouth. They gave her face distinction, and a little softness that had not been there before.

"Doddering?" she said with a small smile, one that reached to her eyes. He wondered how long it had been since something he had said had actually touched her. She continued, "I, too, wish there was something we could do. You know the grounds for the annulment?"

A grimace crossed his features, and he grumbled into his cravat, "Yes. 'Tis obscene, if you ask me. At least you and I tried to make a go of it before . . ." His words trailed away as a stricken look crossed his countenance.

A moment had come upon them, not entirely unexpected, not entirely undesired. Jane took a deep, steadying breath, then came around the low table, sitting next to him, laying a hand over his where it rested on her settee. It was the first time she remembered touching him in years. "Please, let us *not* stop speaking. Let us say what we wish, as we wish. Let us dispel with silence," she said, not quite able to hide her anxiety that he would not continue, that he would stop speaking, again, as always, leaving only silence and hurt between them.

He looked to the ceiling and the walls for a moment or two, but finally he blurted out, "Is it ever too late, Jane? Can two people start over . . . people of our ages?" he asked beseechingly.

Jane smiled shakily, looking into his eyes. "Our ages? Does it matter? Right now I dare to say that I feel very young, very giddy, indeed."

He laughed unsteadily, uncertain yet encouraged. "I know that feeling."

"I'm so glad you came today, Richard," she said, standing and crossing to the double doors that led into the morning room. She closed them gently, turning to lean her back against them. "There is very much that needs to be said, new problems to resolve, old misunderstandings that need to be gotten rid of."

"No time like the present," he said gruffly, as if to make up for the softness that hovered about his features.

"No time, indeed." She crossed the room and found herself in arms that she had been missing in more ways and for more years than she could bear to think.

A week later, Emmeline had pondered a long time. Finally she had come to a decision and had given a house-boy a shilling to carry a discreet note to a certain gentleman.

That evening she assured her sister that she was not feeling up to a ball, and that they must go on without her, and that she would be fine at home with Papa, she only wanted to rest.

As soon as they were gone, Emmeline went upstairs and changed into clothes suitable for nighttime travels. She returned to the downstairs parlor, unlatched the door that led into the gardens, and sat down to wait for her gentleman caller.

Jeffrey stared at his parents, bemused. "That is their

fourth dance together!" he said to Alessandra, blindly handing a glass of punch in her direction.

She hurriedly caught the glass, only a drop or two spilling to the floor and onto her gloves, as the fan hanging from her wrist swung dangerously, threatening to tip even more punch from her unbalanced grip. She righted the glass with her other hand, casting only a mildly exasperated, and largely amused, glance in his direction.

"It would seem they have reconciled some of their differences," Lady Amelia said, trying to reach for the other punch glass he held. He raised it just out of her reach, then absently sipped from it himself.

"Jeffrey," Alessandra almost laughed, "Would you please get Mother some punch?"

"What?" he said, finally taking his eyes off his laughing, smiling parents, only then realizing he was drinking Lady Amelia's punch. "Oh, I see. Beg your pardon! Er, could you hold this until I come back?" He handed the glass to Lady Amelia, and went off to find the punch bowl again.

"Well, he is certainly pleased with events, I must say," Lady Amelia said tartly.

"As am I. It was always so sad, don't you think, the way they were separated?"

"But can they stay together?" Lady Amelia added.

"I hope so," Alessandra sighed with a deeper meaning that went over her mother's head entirely.

When Jeffrey returned, he found his mother-in-law holding two glasses. "Where did Alessandra get off to?" he asked, trading the one glass he had for her for the one from which he had been drinking.

"Von Brauer's got her, for the gavotte," Lady Amelia

said, pointing in the general direction of the dancers.

Jeffrey turned to look where she pointed. "The gavotte? I say, that's terribly old-fashioned, isn't it?"

"So is the Dowager Lady Bremcott, my boy, and this is her ball," Lady Amelia said, without bothering to look repentant for the remark.

"Would you care to join me?" Jeffrey decided all at once, indicating the floor with a movement of his head.

"Delighted!" was the reply.

They found a place to cache the punch glasses, then moved to join the others who were preparing for the dance.

Lady Amelia sighed as she and Jeffrey danced, looking across the floor to where her daughter swayed to the music with the baron as her partner. Alessandra was obviously enjoying herself. She smiled vivaciously up at the man, obviously chatting as the movements of the dance allowed. "They look well together, don't you think? He's not too old for her, is he? Twenty years is a big difference, but that makes him only thirty-eight," she mused.

Jeffrey threw Lady Amelia a startled glance, and when they had the chance, he asked quickly, "What do you mean, ma'am?"

"What do I mean? I'm considering him as husband material, of course." Now it was Lady Amelia who threw the glance, one that was perplexed at his thick-headedness.

Of course, for after the annulment, Jeffrey thought to himself, the frown creasing his forehead inadvertently upsetting the young girl who danced across from him as she wondered what she was doing wrong to make him frown so. *A new husband for Alessandra. Of course. Von Brauer. He is certainly a gentleman, but he is so much older*

223

than she.

Still, that was not enough to disqualify him, Jeffrey knew. Von Brauer had family money, and at least two estates, one in Germany and one in England, and no known heirs. *A quick glance is enough to tell you that Lessie . . . Alessandra likes him,* he thought to himself, frowning even more deeply as he discerned that he had used her pet name without meaning to do so. It had just popped into his brain—probably from being exposed to it so much of late, no doubt.

Still, he could not like her having to live out of the country for part of the year—

What was he thinking? What concern of his was it where she lived, and with whom? Once the annulment was final, they would only meet socially. He would have no need, nor prerogative, to impose what he thought should happen upon her self and her life.

"Jeffrey? Jeffrey?" Lady Amelia said to him, tapping his arm with her fan as they danced.

"Er . . . um . . . yes, ma'am?" He brought his eyes down from watching his wife across the room, her musical laughter coming clearly to his ear, to focus on his mother-in-law.

"I asked you what you think of that fellow over there, the one with too many tassels. Oh, what is his name? His father is the one who married the defunct princess . . . no, she was a princess's lady-in-waiting at one time, I think it was . . . DuBois? Dubonne! That's it! Dubonne. Now, what can you tell me of him? Is there any money in the family? He looks a popinjay to me, but it can at least be said that he is all the crack."

"Slang, ma'am?" Jeffrey said, a little sourly, even though he smiled with the corners of his mouth.

224

"Don't try to scold me. Malcolm has tried for years, to no effect. Well, what do you think of him?"

"He's an idiot, and a gambler. I wouldn't throw my daughter at him, I can tell you that."

She raised her eyebrows at the censure in his tone as their dance ended, but as he led her to the side she decided to resume her questioning concerning the rest of the eligible gentlemen around the room.

He was beginning to become quite annoyed with her by the time Jacqueline came up beside him. He and she had greeted each other when he had entered with Alessandra on his arm at the start of the evening. He had bowed to her, moving past swiftly, not even allowing Alessandra time to do more than nod a greeting to Jacqueline. Now, he turned to the fair blond with a sense of relief, and bid her at once to dance with him.

They would have to wait a few minutes until the previous dance ended, so he led her away at once, directly to the punch bowl as a logical excuse to escape his plaguey mother-in-law with all her questions and comments on prospective beaux.

"Here," he said, shoving a glass into Jacqueline's hand. A cool smile showed that she was mildly vexed at the gracelessness of the moment, but then he was pulling her by the hand into one of the curtained alcoves that faced the ballroom. It was not exactly private, but it did at least provide a little isolation, the very thing he desired most at the moment.

"Thank you," she belatedly said, indicating the punch. Jeffrey was certainly in a strange mood tonight. Should she try to flirt? No, she knew! She would be *concerned:* he seemed to admire that sort of trait, for he was forever popping out with little tales of "Alessandra did this" and "Alessandra said that." "Is anything the matter? I must say it is a bit of a crush in there, but—"

"I'm fine," he said, tugging at his cravat, only to then feel it gingerly to see if he had ruined its set. "Does this look right?" he asked, lifting his chin and leaning down toward her so that she could observe his cravat for him. Alessandra had a knack for setting the lay of his cravat correct after he had mussed it up.

"It looks fine," she said, her look of concern making a noticeable shift toward annoyance. Why did he ask her about his own cravat, instead of commenting on how fetching her pale lime gown was this evening? What of the ribbons and pearls that had been so artfully and painstakingly arranged in her hair? Was the man blind?

The crowd parted for a moment, and Jeffrey, still tugging at his cravat, found himself looking directly at Alessandra as she looked back. It was clear that she had seen him and Jacqueline in the alcove. Her chin lifted, her head turned toward her escort, a Major—the name escaped him—Somebody, and she smiled in a way that could only be called flirtatious.

Really! That is no way for a newlywed wife to act, not to keep up appearances, he thought, instantly aggravated.

"Excuse me," he said curtly to Jacqueline, leaving her standing there gaping after him. The look on her face clearly said that his behavior was just too bad of him, if he had only bothered to look back and see it. He passed the Viscount Aldegard, and some absent part of him knew his lapse in manners well enough that he said to the man in passing, "Lady Bremcott needs a partner. She's in that alcove behind us."

The viscount looked at him, then at the indicated alcove, and made a beeline in her direction.

Jeffrey tapped the Major Somebody on the shoulder, then pushed his way between the man and Alessandra. "My dance," he said, abruptly sweeping Alessandra away, paying no heed to the major's mild protestations. "What are we dancing?" he said out of the side of his mouth to Alessandra, quickly glancing at the other couples, and trying to tell what his steps must be from the music that was just starting.

"A reel."

"Oh, fine. What were you doing?" he said brusquely as the music started, finally turning his countenance to fully face Alessandra.

"Doing?" she asked, honestly perplexed by the question.

"With that major fellow."

"I was preparing to dance with him," she said somewhat tartly, beginning to feel faintly exasperated with Jeffrey. How could she feel any other way when once again he had whisked her into the dance purely at his own whim? This thrill that ran through her at the touch of his hand on hers must be discounted—she must turn it into an effect brought about only by her growing pique at him.

"That's not what I mean. I mean those sheep's eyes you were casting up at him. Really, Alessandra, you must make an attempt to at least appear happily married," he scolded in a low tone, his mouth held close enough to her ear for her to hear, but far enough away that he could look down at her with one disapproving eye.

She blinked several times, her outrage becoming real and growing as each second passed. "I beg your pardon?" she said icily.

"You heard me."

"I had hoped I did not. May I point out to you, sirrah,

that at least I do not secret myself away with young ladies in small, dark alcoves, as *some* we could speak of do. If you want to give lectures on discreet behavior, please talk to yourself!"

The word *discreet* rang a bell in his mind, and he found that he almost lost his place in the dance when he attempted to whip around and stare toward the major, who had found another partner and had joined those already on the floor. "Him?" he cried disbelievingly. "You're planning an affair with him? Why can't you wait?"

Her mouth fell open, and her eyes darted to either side to see if anyone had overheard the incredulous remark. Largely convinced that their awful conversation had gone unheeded, she hissed, "Why can't *you?* You are forever in Lady Bremcott's society. Why can't I find some 'society' if I care to? I am sure I recall our agreement."

"But in a little while you'll be free of me!" he cried, sure his face was starting to turn purple as he fought to suppress this crazy, spinning outrage that was building in his chest.

"Oh . . . ! Oh, hush up!" she cried suddenly, pushing her hands against his chest so that they both stumbled backwards a few steps. She righted herself, then turned on her heel, nearly running in her haste to be away from him, out of his arms.

She disappeared into the crowd as he stared after her. It took him a moment to overcome first his shock, and then the awkwardness of exiting the floor alone past interested gazes, before he began to look for her.

"Lady Huntingsley?" a voice called softly.

Alessandra turned, wiping quickly at her eyes, to note the Baron von Brauer was striding across the lawns toward her.

"It is cold, my dear. May I offer you my jacket?" He started to shrug the garment from his shoulders, but she declined quickly.

"No, I should be going back in. I will . . . in a moment or two."

She turned her back to him, staring up into the night sky as she had been doing until he came along.

"It is most clear dat you are upset," he said, still in that quiet way. "May I be of assistance?"

She gave a small, forced laugh, and answered, "No, but thank you."

"But I tink I could."

She turned at that, regarding him with tears still hovering on her eyelashes. "My lord?" she tried to be polite.

"Customs are different in Germany dan in England. Ve can be very formal vhen ve vish to be, but also sometimes ve know it is better to be less so. You understand vhat I say?"

"No . . ." she answered him hesitantly.

"In England it would be very improper of me to say vhat I vish to say, but vhen I am *der Baron im Deutschland,* then I do as I vish. So, I hereby claim dis little bit of lawn for Germany, for one minute's time."

Her answering smile was fragile.

He came closer to her, taking up her hands. "I haf not been unavare of your mother's interest in me. No, do not fear, she has been discreet, but I am vain enough to admit dat I know vhen a mama is assessing my attributes as a bridegroom. I admit I do not understand dis, as you are

229

married. But do not fear dat I vill ask you for explanations. All I vant to say is dat, your mother's interest aside, it is quite plain to me dat you are in love vit your husband. Und I don't tink he knows dis. You scarcely know it yourself. Dis causes you great pain, and so maybe you tink about other men, you try to divert der mind, but you haf no success. No, my dear girl, don't deny it. Vhy should you?"

"Oh, but I . . . I—" she cried wildly, her heart beginning to pound in her ears at his words.

"I merely vanted to tell you dat dere is no dishonor in love, and dat as he is already your husband dis makes for a tidy resolution, *nicht wahr?* If you vish it, it could be so. *Ja,* you could make it so."

Jeffrey saw her then, her white gown glowing softly in the moonlight, her hands clasped in those of Von Brauer's. Though the fairy lights in the garden barely extended to where they stood, he could tell that her face was flushed as she gazed up at the older man with something like wonder in her expression. Jeffrey's breath seemed to evaporate, and there was a ringing in his ears. He felt as he once had as a lad, in a schoolyard fight, after the blows had knocked him senseless enough that they no longer hurt.

He turned unsteadily on his heel, and marched back into the ballroom. His eyes darted from side to side, as he looked all around, a strange and wild agitation replacing the breathlessness of a moment ago. All at once, the dancing infuriated him, the groups seemed alien and uninviting, and he angrily decided absolutely he would go to find something much stronger than punch to drink.

As he pursued this course with long strides, a hand came out to detain him, catching his sleeve just long enough to stop his forward propulsion. It was Jacqueline, so pretty in her green evening dress, with ribbons and pearls wound through her short blond curls.

"Do you care to dance?" he asked her sharply, abruptly.

She cocked her head at him, puzzled by his tone. She had meant to quietly and softly upbraid him for his earlier abandonment of her, in a manner that could only solicit better attendance on her, but now the peculiar glinting lights in his eyes caused her to lose her determination and merely answer with a calm smile, "That would be lovely."

He took her in his arms, finding it was a waltz. He twirled her about the floor with dizzying speed.

"Please, Jeffrey," she reprimanded him once, concerned they were making a spectacle of themselves.

It was as if he did not hear her. She saw his head turn quickly, heard him suck in his breath sharply. "Look at that!" he growled in her ear. "Von Brauer! . . . and he is having a second dance with Alessandra."

Jacqueline smiled complacently; this suited her to a tee. It was not exactly unseemly that a married lady share a second dance with someone, though it could be pointed out that he was no relative, and it was normally "not done." It just made one more occasion when the other lady had put herself at disadvantage in Jeffrey's eyes.

After the dance, Jeffrey led Jacqueline directly toward the twin pair of doors that someone had opened to let in a little fresh air. Within a moment's time they were outside, her arm entwined in his as they strolled forward, past the fairy lights, out into the unlighted part of the garden.

Jacqueline felt a little tremor course up her spine, for

231

this was the most conspicuous Jeffrey had ever chosen to be with her. A dark garden, no chaperone—it was the setting for love and proposals. Perhaps he had some news of the annulment to share with her; perhaps soon she would be wearing his engagement ring.

She stopped, pulling gently on his arm to arrest his forward propulsion. He seemed distracted, agitated, looking down at her only as they came to a halt. She saw that he stared down at her, but in the darkness she could not read his expression. She waited for either words or actions from him, but neither were forthcoming.

It was still chilly at night, and she began to shiver a little. "Jeffrey, I'm cold," she said, and then, feeling suddenly inspired and emboldened, she turned in to him, pressing against his body.

He remained still, a picture of the tawdry woman he had recently hired flashing through his mind, for she had pressed her body against his in such a fashion. Still, this was Jacqueline, undeniably so because of the faint highlights that the moon picked out in her hair, her familiar scent of lavender wafting on the night breeze. Suddenly he bent his head and found her mouth, kissing her roughly. She whimpered and leaned in to him even more.

As suddenly as the kiss had come, it ended, as he tore his mouth from hers. Yet another flash had gone through his mind, the one where he told himself he might as well be kissing his own brother. There was no spark, no delight in this stolen moment, no thudding of the heart, nothing. Just as the kiss in her garden had been. He pushed her away, staring down into the face he could only faintly make out in the moon's light.

He understood, quite clearly and abruptly, why he had never offered for her, why he had put off thinking of the day, unable to picture her as his wife. She was like a sister to him. Her family had lived next to his all his life, and though he loved her after a fashion, there was nothing passionate or compelling about it. A vision of a future world of missed chances and despondency, of bitterness and regret, flashed in front of his eyes, and he shook his head, shaken by the facts before him. Yes, he knew what a kiss was supposed to do . . . how even the near possibility of a kiss should be making him feel. He knew that he could kiss Jacqueline a hundred times and never come close to what had happened when he . . . when he had held . . . when blue eyes gazed back at him . . . when. . . .

No, never Jacqueline. No.

"Jacqueline," he said softly after a minute's stunned silence. He tried to think how to tell her what he had discovered. All he could think to say, that would not be cruel or unkind, was, "I have decided that I don't want to marry anyone . . . after the annulment. I think you should consider the Viscount Aldegard."

Now it was her turn to be stunned. First the broken kiss, the strange way he had thrust her away, and now this! "Wh-what?" she stammered.

"I'm sorry, but I mean it. Truly. I cannot offer for you."

"Why not?" she cried, her voice rising.

He tried to form some words, but none came to his lips. His mind was too busy trying to sort out his own confused feelings. He finally fell back on a line he had once read in a book, "Because I am not good enough for you."

She stood very still, her offended pride clear to see even through the gloom. Her voice started out low, but it steadily grew in tenor as she cried, "Jeffrey Huntingsley, you have ignored me all evening. You abandoned me and

233

pawned me off on another gentleman as though I were a mere cit." She took a deep breath, as though to steady herself, and went on, "You married that other woman, putting me in the position of having to lower my expectations to becoming what the Ton would call a . . . a *second* wife!" she stammered over the words in her anger, as if they were the ultimate insult. "I've suffered all of this kind of insulting behavior for months, and you tell me it was for *nothing?*" she cried at last. With a furious heave of her breast, she stamped her foot, and cried, "You are quite right: you are *not* good enough for me!" She turned to leave, but then whipped around to add, "Even after I marry the richest, cleverest, most handsome man in London, I don't know if even then I will ever speak to you again, *Lord* Huntingsley!"

She gave him her back, turning and striding away militantly, her dignity held before her like a sword.

For a minute longer he stood there, biting his lip, his empty arms crossed over his chest. He tried to sympathize with the hurt feelings she must be smarting from, but the truth was not too far behind the guilt, for he had to comprehend that she was not truly wounded. There had been no tears, no pleading, only wounded pride.

It was the kindest thing he could have done for both of them, he thought with a huge, relieved sigh.

By the time he arrived back in the ballroom, he saw that Jacqueline was already in the arms of another partner. He had to laugh somewhat to himself, for the fellow she had taken up with was one of the richest men in England.

"Jeffrey?"

He looked around, and smiled when he saw it was his

mother who hailed him. She came close and slipped her arm through his.

"Why do you smile to see Jacqueline flirting so outrageously?" she asked. He looked into her eyes, bright, shining, no longer haunted with sadness, though now they were full of concern for him.

"Mother," he said, his tone somewhere between chagrin and a funny sort of amusement at himself, "The Lady Jacqueline Bremcott and I have decided to *not* have an understanding."

Her eyes widened. "You had a tiff?"

"We had a breaking-off. I will never marry her, Mother, and I doubt I could win her back if I wanted to, which I don't."

"Ah," she said, looking to the girl, then back to her son curiously. "I cannot say I disapprove. So then, do you plan to continue with the annulment?"

He froze beside her, then laughed at himself out loud, a tight, uncertain sound. "I admit I had not gone that far in my thinking. But I do not forget your advise."

"My advise?"

"That it is better to get out of something than let it turn into something you regret."

Her face clouded over, and she asked, "So you still regret marrying Alessandra?"

He frowned, opened his mouth, shut it, then opened it again to speak. "'Regret' is not the correct word," he said carefully.

She sighed, and wistfully said, "I have a regret, Jeffrey."

"What is that, Mother?" He squeezed her hand, for she sounded so somber.

There was something new in the gaze she raised to

his—an openness that had not been there in a long time, a milder shadow of what he had seen the other day. "I regret that I hardened my heart to your father. I never gave him a chance, back then, so early on. I told myself that he could not possibly want to be with me, until I had made it true." She held his gaze steadily, her brown eyes soft with feeling. "It was the biggest mistake I ever made. But now, perhaps, he and I have righted that error. So I feel as though I can tell you this: don't throw away this marriage. Get to know her, talk to her about all that's been between you. Maybe even court her a little, to see if any attraction lies between you. If there is nothing there, then that is the time to go ahead with dissolving the marriage. But don't cast it aside just because it might have seemed the thing to do, once."

"You have become a romantic, or you've been talking to Father Ainsley, for that is much of what he has advised. But, Mother, yesterday you were pleased enough that I was to end up with Jacqueline," he said, shaking his head tolerantly, troubled by the way her words struck a chord inside his chest.

"Was I? I wonder. I wanted what you wanted. I wanted you to have what would make you happy, I know that."

"I need time to clear my head," he declared suddenly. "I need to get away from this place. Will you bring Alessandra home?"

She nodded her head graciously. "I will tell her you have gone."

"Thank you, Mother," he said with heartfelt sincerity. The night had been too much, too crazy. He wasn't sure what he thought anymore, what he felt.

As he rode home, the gentle swaying of the carriage and the clatter of the wheels over the cobblestones lulled

236

his mind into some semblance of order.

So. The subject of Jacqueline could now have a period put cleanly behind it. She was not a part of his considerations anymore. Good. Fine. But what of the rest of the evening? What peculiar and outrageous moments had driven him to leave the company, the moments that had left him feeling so agitated? There had been the incredulous scene of his parents laughing, chatting, dancing . . . a miracle, to his mind. Then there had been Lady Amelia, chatting to him about possible suitors for Alessandra; the ridiculous Dubonne fellow; those scenes of Lessie with Von Brauer, dancing with him, in his arms, or holding his hands in the gardens, out there almost beyond the lights. What of that Major Somebody, with his dashing uniform, the man she had said something about "being discreet" with? And overshadowing them all, his uncharacteristic response to each and every incident.

Why had he been upset by Von Brauer or the major? Why did the picture of her gazing so earnestly up at the baron, her petite form standing in the man's moonshadow, make a growl begin to form in the back of his throat even just to think of it?

Why had his mother's words set a tune playing inside his chest, the sound of one long, clear tone, like the overlong piping of a single flute note? Why did the thought of returning to the Sapphire Room, assuming the cousinly role he had been playing for weeks, suddenly seem so distasteful, so idiotic? Why did a pair of blue eyes, a softly spoken word, a face gentled by slumber, a selfless kindness extended—why did these things superimpose themselves over every other thought he had?

Because he had been an idiot. A blind idiot, unable to see beyond what had been his original expectations. Elias

237

had accused Jacqueline of being a dull, boring pattern card, but he was wrong, for it was Jeffrey that had let circumstances dictate to him time and time again, regardless of the truths that lay before him.

He rapped his cane on the ceiling of the carriage, and when the vehicle came to a halt, he opened the door and leaned out to shout up to the driver, "St. Dennis's Church."

"At this 'our, milord?" the coachman cried back.

"If you please."

"Crazy cove," the coachman muttered without any true malice, shaking his head and giving the horses a flick with the lines.

Inside the carriage, Jeffrey had come to a number of conclusions; he knew what he had to do, and the trip to St. Dennis's church was merely the first.

Chapter 18

"Ah, so this is where you got yourselves off to instead of the Bremcott Ball," Jeffrey greeted Elias and Emmeline.

They looked up with guilty faces from the chessboard between them, and they each cried, "You are home early!"

"Where is Alessandra?" Emmeline added.

"Mother and Father are bringing her home. Why are you dressed to go out, Emmeline?" Jeffrey asked casually.

"Jeffrey, there is something I need to tell you." Elias darted a quick look at Emmeline, who flushed dark red and leapt up from her chair.

"I . . . I need to . . . to go . . . to bed!" she cried, finally finding an uninspired excuse.

"Good night," Jeffrey said, his tone and his expression both patently amused.

"Good night, all," she trilled in a manner very unlike her normal self, then she practically ran from the room, with Elias's unnaturally bright eyes watching, it would appear longingly, as she made her departure.

After a moment, Elias turned to his older sibling, his face pale despite the two bright spots of color on his cheeks, and said straight out, "Jeffrey, old bean, there's nothing for it but to tell you that I've been a very bad fellow."

"Yes, I know, and you had Emmeline as your accomplice," Jeffrey said matter-of-factly, even as he grinned wolfishly at his brother.

"What . . . what is it you think I've done?" Elias asked, subconsciously taking a step backward beyond his brother's reach.

"I happen to know you've gone to Father Ainsley and told him that Lessie and I have been sharing a room."

At first Elias's face went a shade more pale, but then his eyes narrowed a little with his more usual cunning. He questioned, "So she's 'Lessie' now, is she?"

Jeffrey cocked his head a little to one side, saying nothing, still smiling enigmatically.

"So this means you have gone to see the good father yourself—but why?"

"I, and you, were not the only ones to see him. It might surprise you to know that Mother and Father also shared the news with the good father. He tells me he is heartily sick of the lot of us, visiting him at all hours of the day and night, constantly contradicting one another. But I digress: you asked me 'why.' I went there to clear the air, of course."

"What?"

"Good night, brother. We'll talk tomorrow."

"What?" Elias cried again, completely dumbfounded.

Jeffrey just laughed; it was so rare to have the upper hand with Elias, he really could not help himself.

Elias went at once to Emmeline's room, reporting the details of how the confession had gone forward, although his retelling was more confusing than the original version, as he grew more perplexed and mystified as he had time to consider what had been said. As he stood at her door, his whisper dropping off in equal proportions to the growing scowl of concentration on his face, Jeffrey came down the corridor. They ceased at their whispering at once, and acknowledged his nod with ones of their own. They stared after him as he went down the stairs. At once, they resumed their tête-à-tête, only to be interrupted a few minutes later as Jeffrey returned, this time with a basket on his arm.

He stopped before them, and said, "When Alessandra returns, will you be so kind as to tell her to come up to the Sapphire Room?" He started to go, but then he turned and added, "You play the pianoforte, don't you, Emmeline?"

They both nodded, mutely.

"Would you be so good as to start playing loudly when I pound three times on the balcony rail?"

Again she nodded mutely, and they both stared after him as he turned to go down the upper corridor to his room. Then they looked at each other, utterly perplexed.

"I'll wait for Lessie," Emmeline decided at once, coming from her room and closing the door behind herself.

"I hope we didn't just kill this marriage," Elias half-whispered in a worried voice.

Emmeline said nothing, her eyes also full of that very concern.

*　　　*　　　*

"Alessandra!" Emmeline called to her, coming from the chair she had positioned directly before the front door, rising to meet her sister in a high state of agitation.

Alessandra looked up from where she had been cheerlessly watching one foot shuffle itself before the other. She was on the verge of tears, and she did not want to talk to anyone, not even Emmeline.

Aunt Jane and Uncle Richard came in behind her, having told Mr. Cloch that they would announce themselves. Emmeline glanced at the pair, more than a little perturbed to see them there, now. "Thank you for bringing Lessie home," she said with the barest hint of politeness. "Are your horses waiting?" she added with little grace.

"I'm not going anywhere, Emmeline. I wish to speak with my son," Jane said sternly.

Emmeline looked directly at Alessandra. "Jeffrey asked that you come at once up to the Sapphire Room," she said. Her handwringing manner implied that the request had not been a casual one, and also that Aunt Jane was not going to see her son soon.

Alessandra looked toward the stairs, one tear sliding down her cheek. She raised a hand and wiped it away, the dejected tears that teetered on her lashes filling eyes suddenly grown angry. What did he want? What would he have to say? It was not bad enough that he had left her at the ball without a word, but on the ride home Aunt Jane had told her that he had broken off his relationship with Jacqueline. How humiliating! The whole world knew their business, and he did not even have the grace to tell her himself. And this, just after the baron had made her see what she had tried so hard not to see. What did it mean now, this newly realized love? How could she

242

have been so stupid as to fall in love with the one man she never should have? Jeffrey had made it clear that he wanted nothing to do with her. His inadvertent acts of attraction meant nothing, no matter how she tried to make them do so, for had he not always turned away in the end? Now, he undoubtedly wanted to tell her that he still wanted the annulment, Jacqueline or no. Well, that was no surprise. How could it be, after all these weeks of rejection?

He would have his annulment, and the sooner the better.

"Lessie? Are you all right?" Emmeline cried, her hand to her mouth as she took in the conflicting emotions that raced across her sister's face.

"Yes," Alessandra said curtly. She was all right, and she would remain so, she decided resolutely. It was no longer necessary to fool the servants; it was time the "marriage" began to "fall apart." Tonight she would move back to her old room, and her father could yell and rant until he was blue, but to no avail. Her mind was made up.

"Lessie, I fear I have made a grievous error—" Emmeline began to explain.

"Tomorrow, Emmeline," Alessandra said in a voice made harsh by choked back tears. "Whatever it is, you may explain it to me tomorrow."

Emmeline and her aunt and uncle looked at one another, equally rocked by the grim resolution they heard in Alessandra's voice.

"We . . . we need some tea, I think," Jane cried, crossing the room to take Emmeline's arm in hers. "Come," she said in a quiet but inarguable tone, "let us leave them to come to terms. There is naught we can do

243

for them now."

"What did we do, going to that Father Ainsley fellow?" Uncle Richard asked the tops of his boots as he followed the ladies in the direction of the kitchens.

Alessandra moved up the stairs, her white skirts trailing behind her like the tail of a comet, her head held high, her mouth set in grim determination. She had neglected to light herself a candle, but her anger carried her along on feet that knew the way. This could only be the final trip to the Sapphire Room, a room she had come to know well and which she felt she could only forevermore loathe.

She came down the hallway, stopping before the closed door to the room, where she took a deep, quavering, fortifying breath of air before she reached for the door handle. Just as her hand touched the knob, a pair of hands came out of the darkness, lightly encircling her waist. She pivoted quickly, the breath of air becoming a gasp, and then a pair of lips met hers.

For an instant she was frightened, but just as swiftly she knew it was Jeffrey who was holding her, pressing his mouth to hers. In anger mixed with confusion and wonderment she allowed him to kiss her.

He knew it was bad of him to wait for her like this, coming from out of the darkness, but he had to know, he had to have an honest reaction.

After several hard thuds of her beating heart, after she tasted hunger and desire and things she could not name on his lips, he started to pull away, and she found her hands at his lapels and then around his neck, her fingers caressing the ends of his hair. She knew she was losing her anger, no, more than that she was losing her head; she wanted him to not pull away, to kiss her again. Oh, she was mad, mad, not only to allow him to do this, but to encourage it.

At her touch, he leaned into her, pressing her back against the door, his strength measured against hers, his neck bending down to renew the touch of his lips on hers. She felt her anger slipping away, burning into ashes, bitter ashes that should remind her of his fickleness, his uncaring. She felt her traitorous lips responding to his, her body smoothing into the lines of his where they met.

One part of her cried out to go on kissing him, to give herself to him under any circumstances, but another part still smarted from the humiliations of being uncherished and left behind. Slowly, almost unwillingly, she forced her mouth away from his, her hands sliding down from his neck to once again rest on the lapels of his jacket. She could feel his heart pounding under her hand, its cadence matching her own.

"Jeffrey, no," she whispered, hot tears springing to her eyes.

"You kissed me back." It did not sound like an accusation; in fact, the words sounded almost triumphant, jubilant. Oh, how could he tease her so cruelly?

Suddenly he moved, and she almost stumbled backwards, for he had unlatched the door at her back. Just as quickly, he scooped her up in his arms, and carried her through the doorway, kicking the door to behind them.

On the other side, he stopped, continuing to hold her, and with a glitter in his eye that was picked out by the fires in the grates, his mouth came down on hers again. He kissed her long and hard, demandingly. She could do nothing but respond, kissing him back, her hands in his hair, touching his face, marveling at the feel of him, there, kissing *her*, holding *her*. It was the sweetest torture

245

she had ever known, and it was quietly breaking her heart.

Finally, he raised his head, an almost drunken look on his face. He shook his head, like a dog shaking off water, and grinned at her, and she felt her poor, battered heart turn over yet again, for it was that special smile of his.

"What is happening?" she asked desperately.

He moved to set her in a chair before the nearest fireplace, and went down to one knee in front of her. "Alessandra," he said, then smiled softly, and amended in a low voice, "Lessie."

She thought she was going to cry, but she had to listen to him, had to concentrate on his words. There was something . . . encouraging . . . in the way he said her name; it had almost sounded like a caress.

"Lessie, I have been the world's biggest fool."

She shook her head slightly, completely at sea as to what was happening, though a note, strong and clear and hopeful, seemed to be growing inside her head, ringing through her brain.

"I am never going to marry Jacqueline Bremcott. Even if I had never met you, I would never have ended up making her my wife. But I *am* glad I met you, and I will tell you why. To do so I must also tell you that I tried to kiss Jacqueline tonight, and that it was a miserable failure. You see, my dear, I have come to realize that the only pair of lips I want near mine are yours."

Her heart plummeted and then rose again, as she stared into his face questioningly.

"Like this," he said, leaning forward to kiss her again.

When he pulled away, despite herself, she cried in painful honesty, "I am terrified that you are saying you

246

want me because you can no longer have Jacqueline Bremcott."

"Jacqueline Bremcott be demmed! I don't love her. I love *you!*"

"How could you possibly?" she whispered.

He laid his head in her lap, his shoulders slumped in agonized laughter. After a moment he raised it again, his face filled with care curiously mixed with that same jubilance that had been in his voice earlier. Coming to his feet and pulling her to hers, he said, "Come."

He pulled her gently toward a table he had set up in the middle of the room. On it were set lighted candles, an opened bottle of wine, a loaf of bread, some sliced meat and cheese, a tray of fruit. "Your seat, my lady," he said, formally handing her into her chair.

"Jeffrey, what is—?"

"We did not have a courtship. You will now allow me to court you."

She lowered her eyes shyly to the food, a thrill running through her, one she could not, must not trust.

"Wine, my lady?" he asked, pouring some into her goblet with a flourish. "What do you think of the weather lately?" he asked as he took his own seat.

She could only sit there, silently staring at him from wide eyes.

"Yes, it has been a bit damp, but there is definitely a warming trend." He picked up an apple and began slicing it into thin slices, some of which he reached across to settle on her plate. She dropped her eyes, watching his hand—a fine, noble, gentleman's hand—and found she could not raise her eyes again, for she knew he would see that she was trembling if she did. "And Napoleon is still being a bad fellow, isn't he? Yes, quite. Leaving Elba, and all that. Oh, the Regent—quite a scandal, I do agree. Yes, I heard about the new bay at the races yesterday, and I think I shall have to go and see her lines for myself. Of course you may go with me; 'twould be my delight," he rambled on, until he saw a ghost of a smile appear on her down-turned face at his banter.

He reached across the table, lifting her chin with his hand, forcing her to meet his look. "There. I think we have exhausted all the current conventional bits. Let's move on to the part where I get to woo you."

"This is so hard to believe," she whispered.

He came around the table at once, on one knee before her again and said, "Believe it."

"Your change of heart is so sudden. . . ."

"It is not. I was falling in love with you the minute those blue eyes looked down the aisle of the church at me. Now the only doubt I have is: whether you think you could ever fall in love with me?" he asked, hope in every syllable, his hands gathering up hers.

"I . . ." she faltered. Could he say such things if he didn't mean them? How many times had she thought she had seen some sign of regard from him, only to be crushed and hurt anew each time? Or had those moments been what he would now have her think they had been? Had he been quietly, secretly falling in love with her? Had he reprimanded her at the ball because he did not like to see her in another man's arm? Had he dashed off to that alcove with Jacqueline Bremcott in order to hurt her in return? And what the Baron von Brauer had said . . . the baron had told her that she loved her husband, a fact she could not deny once it was uttered aloud. Was there any possible way that Jeffrey could love her as well? Was there any possible way that her secret, unspoken dream could be coming true?

Now was the time to find out.

She spoke quickly, before her courage could fail her. "I think I have been falling in love with you all along."

"Then you were quite wrong not to let me know. Both of us were terribly wrong. What a perfect pair of fools are we," he teased her softly, his eyes dancing as his hands tightened on hers. "Lady Huntingsley," he said formally, his chin rising high, "would you do me the honor of being my wife?"

What if she were wrong? What if he was only settling for second best? But why should he be? He could have told her very clearly, very easily that he still intended the annulment go through. It would have been very simple. It had been what she had expected when she came up those stairs. There was no reason to keep her as his bride, no reason at all.

Except one.

She looked up with eyes that were at last filled with serenity, with a wordless elation sprung from a newborn certainty that could only be silently, joyously, reflected in her face. "Yes," she whispered, and then his lips were crushing hers, and she was free to hold him, without any reservations.

He kissed her over and over again, her pins falling from her long dark hair, allowing the length of it to tumble down her back and become entwined in their embraces. He murmured endearments and half-worded explanations, and he told her that she was never, ever to dance with the Baron von Brauer again. She did not fully understand his insistence, but she laughed joyously, knowing that one day she must thank the baron for helping her to arrive at this moment.

His arms disentangled from about her, and he murmured in a low voice, "Excuse me."

With dismay she saw him leave the room. She heard him run along the corridor, and then there was a pounding on the stairs' railing, and he came running back.

"Listen!" he explained when he closed the door again, crossing at once to pull her up from the chair and into his arms, where he kissed her again, putting any newly arisen anxieties to rest at once. "Would you care to dance, my dear?"

Faintly she heard the strains of a waltz coming from the pianoforte downstairs, and she melted into his embrace as he led her through the dance. She felt giddy, as though she'd had a half-dozen glasses of wine, more so with each kiss he rained down upon her, their bodies close, more intimate than they could ever be in any ballroom.

The music ended, and she felt once again his heart beating under her hand where it lay on his coat. He stood very still, then scooped her up in his arms once again, carrying her to the bed. "Please tell me," he said in a low, beseeching tone, "that we may now use the middle of this sagging mattress as it was intended to be used."

"A wife should never argue with her husband," she said demurely, letting her arms wrap around his neck once more, rejoicing when she heard his deep-chested laughter.

"James!" Emmeline cried. She leaped up from a concerned gathering of low-voiced family members to fly

250

across the room to her husband. "What are you doing here? I'm so happy you've come!"

"My job with the Consulate is completed, so I returned home early, only to find my wife has been gone this month past," he said, no less cheery for all the traveling he had done this day to arrive in London. He gave her a big hug in return, and kissed her soundly on the mouth, despite the fact there were several witnesses in the room.

Her mother and father looked on with tolerance, but Elias grinned at the sight.

"You remember Cousin Elias, don't you, James? He was at our wedding," Emmeline made the introductions. "And this is Lord and Lady Chenmarth, Alessandra's father and mother-in-law."

James's eyebrows rose at the information that his sister-in-law was now in a position to have in-laws of her own. After greeting Lord and Lady Hamilton, James extended his hand to Lord Chenmarth, saying, "My lord, we have met before, over a billiard table. As I recall, you are quite wicked with a cue stick."

"I have heard that he likes to play late at night. I wonder if he will still play as often?" Jane said with a secret smile and a loving look toward her husband, who blushed but then looked equally like the cat who has been at the cream. James knew at once that the little scene would have to be explained to him in private, and at a much later time.

"Elias, old man. How are you?" he said, taking up the other man's hand for a quick shake.

"Well enough, unless my brother kills me," was the answer.

"Is that likely?" James asked, no sign of amusement on his usually deceptively somber face, a face that leant

251

itself well to government service. He had enough experience to know that the sensation that had struck him when he came in the room had been one of some tension.

"'Fraid so."

"It's a long story, I'll explain it all to you later, but suffice it to say that Alessandra has married, and she and he are not on best terms," Emmeline said quickly. "In fact, we were just consulting with Mama and Papa as to what should be done."

"Done? Isn't it up to Alessandra and this husband of hers to do anything?"

"Well, yes, except that there was," she glanced guiltily at Elias and the Chenmarths, and then at the floor, "some meddling."

James almost laughed at her blatant self-incrimination, but settled for shaking his head.

"Why did you have to go talk to the vicar?" Lord Malcolm gloomily asked the room at large.

Lady Amelia looked at him with a censure that said it was all but a case of the pot calling the kettle black, but she merely said, "I think we ought to check on them." It was clear, though, that she had really rather not.

"I shall feel awful, simply awful, if we have spoiled things for them," Jane said with feeling, earning a nodding agreement from Richard.

"They have been up there a long time. They've probably killed each other. You're right, Amelia, let us go and talk to them, if they're still alive," Lord Malcolm said.

"What, disturb them in their room?" James cried, aghast.

"Oh, James, you don't understand," Emmeline assured him, trailing at once after her parents.

James and Elias looked at each other, but when Elias shrugged, they both headed for the stairs at once.

At the top of the stairs they were met by Patty, in a voluminous robe over her nightwear, and Winters, still dressed, in clothes that looked as if he had been napping in them.

"Wot's amiss?" Patty asked her employer. "I couldn't sleep fer the sound of carriages arriving and doors a'slamming. Why didn't someone ring fer me, ta fetch a tray?" she said in deep censure when she saw all the guests standing on the landing.

"Is his lordship to home then?" Winters asked at the same time. "He never rang for me."

Lord Malcolm waved aside their questions, giving a hushed cry of "Enough!" and all but tiptoed to the door of the Sapphire Room. He knocked gently, almost as if he really did expect to find dead bodies on the other side. There was no answer. He knocked again, more loudly, and still there was no answer. He put his hand to the latch, and finding it gave easily, he cast a wary look around the group clustered outside the door, then turned the knob and pushed the door open.

There was a sort of scene of carnage inside the room: clothes were scattered about without a thought toward their care, food was left uneaten on a table that was strangely in the middle of the room, and lamps had been carelessly left burning. But what made the entire entourage gasp was when they saw two bodies on the bed, their limbs, which could be guessed to be without benefit of clothing, entwined. They were both soundly asleep.

Lord Malcolm leapt back, pulling the door closed with

wide eyes and a hanging jaw. Lady Amelia raised her cool hands to touch her warm face, everlastingly grateful that Oliver was sound asleep in his bed; Jane coughed delicately; Richard coughed loudly in embarrassment; Patty winked at Winters, who gave her back an equally gratified glance that brought a blush to her cheeks; Emmeline stared at James, who looked around at the others as though they had all come directly from bedlam; and Elias gave a gigantic, exultant whoop.

With a universal effort at shushing Elias, they all moved with a belated respect for privacy toward the stairs, until the door to the Sapphire Room was yanked open again. Jeffrey stood there in his robe, his feet, legs, and chest obviously bare beneath it. "What's going on?" he asked sleepily.

"Nothing. Go back to my daughter," Lord Malcolm said gruffly, even as he colored up all the way to his gray-streaked hairline.

Jeffrey's eyebrows raised, and he observed his copiously grinning brother in the group.

"Does this mean no Jacqueline? No annulment?" Elias cried, unable to stop himself.

Jeffrey blinked the sleep from his eyes as he appeared to ponder his brother's questions to make some sense of them, but then he grinned slowly in return. "No annulment. Ever," he said firmly.

"Did *we* do this?" Elis cried, pointing at Emmeline, Lady Jane, Lord Richard, and himself. He would have gone forward to talk to his brother, but James quickly put a hand on his shoulder, holding him back.

"Of course not. Jeffrey and I did," Alessandra said, poking her head out the door around her husband's side.

Her smile was suitably shy despite her provocative words.

Lady Amelia looked as though she would faint, but Jane finally could not hold back her much-satisfied smile.

"I told you it would work to put them together!" Lord Malcolm cried to his wife, grabbing her and doing a spontaneous jig, bringing the color back into her face as he forced her to hop about with him.

"Well, at least we shall not have to return the wedding gifts," Amelia said as she held on to her husband's arms to keep from losing her balance. She slowly began to smile. "Oh, stop!" she said, referring to the jig, then laughed, and danced a few more steps with him.

"Go to bed. We certainly wish to," Jeffrey said, still grinning. They all saw him pull his wife to his side, plant a kiss on her happily upturned face as he pushed the door shut, and heard the key turning decidedly in the lock, followed by a trill of feminine laughter.

"May I assume that Jeffrey Huntingsley is Alessandra's husband?" James asked the group that moved to file down the stairs.

They all stared at him, then burst into laughter, and poor James was never allowed to forget that he had ever asked such a witless question.

Inside the room, Jeffrey asked, "Who was that fellow that kindly kept Elias from invading our sanctum?"

"My sister's husband, James."

"Ah. Never having spoken one word with him, I am already convinced that I like him very much." He touched her nose with one finger playfully, and asked,

"Did you hear your father's triumphant statement?"

"I am afraid we have broken our cousinly contract."

"So we have," he said, his face serious, his eyes dancing.

"You realize that Papa will forever be reminding us that he was correct about what would happen if he made us share this room. Given that, you don't wish Papa had been wrong and you had remained right, do you?" Alessandra asked, affecting a hurt pout that was completely at odds with the smile in her eyes.

"Good heavens, no," he said as he wrapped his arms about her and proceeded to show her how completely content he was to have proven himself quite mistaken.